I0647346

The Mosaic V

A COMPILATION OF SHORT STORIES

EDITED BY: DR. CASSUNDRA WHITE-ELLIOTT

This book contains works of both non-fiction and fiction. In the cases of fictional writings, the stories may have been fashioned after true stories but are not exact retellings.

CLF Publishing, LLC.
9161 Sierra Ave, Ste. 203C
Fontana, CA 92335
www.clfpublishing.org

Copyright © 2017 by Cassundra White-Elliott. All rights reserved. No portion of this book may be reproduced, stored in a retrieval system, or transmitted by any form or any means electronically, photocopied, recorded, or any other except for brief quotations in printed reviews, without the prior permission of the publisher.

All rights reserved. No portion of this book may be reproduced, stored in a retrieval system, or transmitted by any form or any means electronically, photocopied, recorded, or any other except for brief quotations in printed reviews, without the prior permission of the publisher.

ISBN # 978-1-945102-17-2

Printed in the United States of America.

Dedications

This book is dedicated to all aspiring writers who were told they couldn't make it in the field of writing or who may have been too scared to move forward because of a fear of failure.

The fourteen writers, whose stories are included within, are proof that you can be successful and your dreams can be a reality.

So, I invite you to pursue your own writing and be the success you know you are.

Dr. Cassundra White-Elliott

Acknowledgements

I acknowledge all the participants in this project, who helped to see it from its stages of inception to its complete fruition.

May your success be plentiful, as you continue to pursue your educational and writing endeavors. I look forward to working with each of you individually, collectively, or both, in the near future.

Much love and appreciation,

C. White-Elliott

Dr. Cassundra White-Elliott

Table of Contents

Mariah Halbert

Introduction

Welcome to **The Mosaic**, where you will enter the exciting world of short stories. Here, the imagination can and will unfold right before your very eyes. What you least expect just may become the expected.

The fourteen authors have delved within their own imaginations and pulled out all the stops and barred no holds. Their tales will excite you, cause curiosity to grow, bring tears of sadness, and/or even feelings of wonderment.

They are skillful in their craft, and they are to be congratulated for their efforts. They have stepped into unknown territory with publishing and sharing their talents with the world at large.

So, I invite you to sit back, relax with your favorite drink, curl up in your most comfortable chair and be prepared for the journeys that lie ahead.

With no further ado, I invite you to ENJOY!!!!!!!!!!

Music or Medicine?

Celine Acuna

"This is how the world changes, good people raising their babies right."

~Shonda Rhimes

(Grey's Anatomy)

It had been a mentally exhausting day for me. I had a full day of classes at school, topped off with my Senior Path Planning (S.P.P) appointment with my counselor. For a full hour, I was stuck trying to make a quick decision that I had been dreading since my first day of senior year. I had spent almost all of my senior year thinking about what path to take after high school. You would think I would have made a decision by then, but that was not the case. I did not want to leave my S.P.P paper empty or write down the wrong field of study. Unfortunately, I only had a few more minutes of my group meeting with my counselor. In the first five minutes of the meeting, I noticed some students were answering every question as "undecided."

It was now the last five minutes of our meeting, and I saw some students who were still vigorously writing down their plan for after high school. How could they be so sure of what they wanted to dedicate the next four years of their lives to? I know I had no idea. I was not anywhere close to finishing my S.P.P paper while the kids I envied were completing filling out their dreams and goals for the next four years. Five minutes before the bell rang, I scribbled "undecided' on my paper. I could already feel the regret before I even finished writing out the full word. I just prayed everything would work out in the end.

I got home around 4:00 pm that day, which is later than I normally get home. I took the long way home to give myself some time to think. I did not take my normal shortcut through the loud and lively city park. Instead, I walked down every unnecessary boring sidewalk to my house. As I was walking, I thought about my life after high school. I also thought about my aunt Amy who I so desperately admired and both my mom and dad, Rose and Phil.

My parents were natural born rockers. They met at one of my dad's first gigs back in the day when my dad's band used to be the opener for every big show that came to our small town's summer concerts series. My mom stopped my dad after he was done playing his heart out and criticized his lyrics. She is the kind of woman to offer her opinion even when it is not being asked. I guess my dad liked it because the rest is history. They had me one year later and have been together ever since. My mom now writes the songs for my dad's band. My parents like to say the more their love improves so does their music, and it must be true because my dad is no longer the opening act. Instead, he's the main attraction. After every show, he brings us up on stage to show off his girls.

I know my parents' dream is to have a family band. They have been talking about it since I was kid. We have always held off on starting a family band because my parents want me to focus on my education. Although sometimes my dad lets me play a song or two to settle down the crowd after the show is over, but that is just when my show begins. I am more into soft rock while both my parents are into hard rock. I love showing people what I can do with a guitar in my hands and microphone in front of me, but in my life I have two loves, music and medicine.

"Enough music," I told myself as I tried to think about anything else. Naturally thoughts of medicine and science came into my mind: my other love. I was first interested in medicine when my parents needed a babysitter for an out of town show and asked my aunt Amy to babysit me. Amy is a research neurologist and has focused the last seven years of her career on Alzheimer's. Along with every other kid my age, I hated the hospital. Hospitals were always so cold and depressing, not to mention all the sick people. I was paranoid of catching something from someone.

Instead, that day I fell in love. I watched Amy work her magic all night. First, through a microscope; then, she typed away her life in a paper, and lastly, she made a presentation that would have blown my socks off if I were not wearing sandals. I know it sounds boring. What freshman in high school would get so passionate about science? Well, I did. That night, I started to dream big and wild. I dreamed of working alongside my aunt or continuing her work. I dreamed of having my name published in a medical journal or even school textbooks. I started to imagine my name inside a science book.

Most high school students don't care about the published names in their textbooks. I know I for one never did but still the thought of it just brought so much excitement to me! I like to believe some of my aunt's passion rubbed off on me. Since I am an only child, we are very close. I decided to call her on my walk home, mostly to get the latest details on her labs, but she would soon sense that something was troubling me. Amy said something to me that only Amy could say, "Follow your heart, but do not forget your brain that tells your feet to follow." Only Amy could come up with a line like that; she is a neurologist after all. Unfortunately, I was too stressed to take her advice.

When I finally got home, I went into my parent's home studio to unwind. Since I did not have a lab at home, I figured some music would calm me down. I was surrounded by my parents' passion for music. On the walls, there were countless album pictures and all the variations of my dad's band shirts, dating back to the early 80's. My mom decorated the room with her lyrics painted on the walls, and in the corner of the room was a broken guitar in a showcase from a time when my dad got a little too much into the music.

My favorite thing about the studio has always been a blown up picture of me as a baby. I was at a show with my parents wearing a baby onesie with the logo of my dad's band Sayer. In the picture, my mom is holding me while my dad is trying to retrieve his guitar pick from my drooling teething mouth. How could my parent's only child not want to be a musician like them? Music is amazing and wonderful. It is so full of life and love, but medicine actually sustains life. Both of them are so fulfilling and rewarding to me. Since I couldn't work out my problem with a scientific formula, I decided to start playing.

I'm not a songwriter like my mom, but that day the words just came to me. Somehow singing about a girl who is torn in two inspired me to talk to my parents. My dad had another show that night like he normally does on Fridays. I had it all planned out. I would tell my parents after the show when they were in a good mood. That is every teenager's plan for approaching his/her parents anyway, right?

Finally, the time came. My parents were packing up all the band equipment after a long show. My dad had sweat dripping down his face, and my mother was still rocking to the songs in her head. Some of the crowd was still hanging out socializing. The crowd was a mixture of unique hair-dos, tattoos, piercings, and personalities. I looked at my own parents who blended in with their fans, unlike me. My mom always had purple hair. Every photo I have ever seen of her, she is rocking her purple locks, and my dad does not believe in haircuts or shaving. His hair has been longer than mine one too many times. That is something he prides himself on while I try to ignore his "accomplishments." One look at me, and you would think I was attending my first show ever. However, I have been to well over a hundred shows in my short lifetime.

My trance was surprisingly broken by my own voice, my singing to be exact. The crowd was calmly swaying to my song I was singing earlier. I looked to my parents, and they both flashed me a big smile. I then looked at the big screen projector hanging above the stage, and there was a video of me singing earlier in our home studio. I should have known they were listening to me sing. They always were just a little too proud of me. I wanted to be upset, but I could not. I was too awestruck by the crowd's reaction to my music. Things just got a lot more complicated.

I needed a pep talk if I was going to talk to my parents. I called Amy yet again. With her advice, I was able to muster up some courage. "Mom... Dad ... I need to tell you something." I swear I planned out my speech better in my head, but once I started talking, I could not stop. Words kept spewing out of my mouth without my permission. Was I offending them? Were they upset? It did not matter at the time. I needed my parents to understand my love for medicine and need for reason and logic. I love the feeling of working hard on a formula and finding the answer. I have so many dreams. One of them is to work side by side with my aunt. My biggest dream in life is to be one of the first doctors to start to fully treat Alzheimer's. I want to help improve my patients' neurological lives. I can't control my excitement when I think about removing my first brain tumor. At the end of my speech, all I could do was pray again, "Dear Lord, please help me… because I am pretty sure I just raised my voice at my mom."

My mother was the first to embrace me in her arms. She was followed right by father like clockwork. Were my parents really hugging me right after I crushed their dreams of a family band and so much more? I stood still in shock of my parents' approval. Everything I had been worrying about for the last year was gone. I felt a rush of relief and happiness beyond compare. I felt as if I just found the cure for Alzheimer's. I couldn't wait to call Amy and tell her, but first I rocked my heart (and brain) out with my parents.

That night, I sang my heart out on stage to my parents. I was excited to start my medical education after high school, and I felt so much comfort knowing I could always come home to jam with my parents. The beat of the music left no room in my heart for the regret that I was feeling earlier that day. It felt good knowing that I could return to school on Monday and properly fill out my S.P.P paper. I learned that night that the love I have for music and medicine is nothing compared to the love my parents have for me.

About the Author

Celine Acuna is a student at Crafton Hills College, in California. She is the second oldest child in a family of five. Celine enjoys spending time with her four siblings: Cynthia, Angelica, Gloria and Fernando, when they are not annoying her. When it comes to writing, Celine loves to write to express herself and enhance her writing skills. She also enjoys writing short stories. Celine's mother Angelic has always told her that she is great at making up stories.

"Music or Medicine?" is Celine's first published short story, and she hopes to continue to publish more of her ideas for others to enjoy. In the years ahead, Celine hopes to travel and incorporate her adventures in her writing. Her advice to any new writers is not let anyone's negative reactions or statements steal away your excitement. If no one supports you, then you must support yourself. Celine would like to thank her mother Angelic Jimenez for sharing in her excitement with her and providing her with spiritual guidance.

A Little about a Board Member

Yolanda Castro

"Sometimes you have to realize that the world is too beautiful to waste your time being angry or sad when you could be enjoying what life has to offer."

www.LiveLifeHappy .Com

One experience that I will never forget is running a campaign while going through a divorce. It was the last week before the deadline to pull papers at the Coachella Valley Unified School District. Pulling papers was the easy part, but coming up with $500 for the voter's note was not easy. Running a campaign was one of the greatest decisions I ever made. Teachers were counting on me to run the campaign against three men. Parents and students wanted a change in the district. Trustee Area 1 was the chair I would be running to win. Endorsed by the teachers and supported by the parents and students, I decided to take the challenge.

Just one month for elections, recently endorsed by the teacher's union, I had to give the campaign my all. I had no idea how to run a campaign, but I knew what my heart wanted to follow. Even if it was broken in pieces in my personal life, I was not going to give up on my community. I, along with my four children, was ready for the challenge. I was going to win, beating the odds of competing with three experienced men in the society. My odds of winning the chair were slim. There I was, a mother of four, going through a divorce, and a student at College of the Desert. In my mind, the community would judge me and see me as a poor candidate.

Feelings stirred within me. However, during every interview, I would always put a smile on my face, and I would never give into sad or vulnerable feelings. I presented myself strong and ready for changes in our district. As the campaign race grew tougher and the opponents grew more intense, I remained calm and positive. I did not run a race with malicious rants about the other opponents or by downsizing candidates.

In the November 8 elections, I won with 43% of the vote. Yes, my name was on the ballot along with Hillary Clinton and Donald Trump. It is definitely something to remember always. My only motivation was my children and the district I was about to represent. My closest friends felt I should not run until my personal life was more settled. They expressed their sentiments to me in many ways.

But, I used those comments to motivate myself even more to continue and to give the campaign my all.

One of my friends stated that I must love the district so much to be willing to run at that moment of hostility and bad climate in our district. Our captain, the superintendent, left the boat, (our district) right at the time of elections and commotion. It was up to the new board to grab all the stakeholders together and work with a temporary captain for a while until the new captain arrived.

The first sixty days were not easy having our teachers about to go on strike due to contract negotiations not being settled for the past twenty months. The climate in our district was hostile, with our students walking out of two different schools and our administrators being intimidated and powerless. It was an intense environment to walk into. Luckily, on the Friday before, new Board Members, the teachers, and district were able to come to an agreement. We had to summit the proposal to the Teachers Union to vote on it and then to the county.

After a week of waiting, the board had to approve it. We voted on the contract with a unanimous vote. Our teachers were exited to go on the winter vacation with no worries of going on strike, which was originally planned to take place right after winter break. I was content to hear all the positive feedback from the teachers. Our students were happy as well, along with our community.

Being an elected official is not easy as it looks. One has to see and make the decisions that will be in the best interest of all stakeholders. Sometimes, those decisions will change people's lives forever. It includes deciding who is best and suitable to our students, new adopted programs that need to be purchased, getting all stakeholders on board to make the programs work for everyone. Millions of dollars to be decided upon for the betterment of our district is a tough decision. Some programs might work and some might not. Some people might do their job and some might not. All these decision go to our board to be approved or denied. Many community members might feel they can make better decisions and question board members about them, but I am here to tell you it is not easy being in that position. As I mentioned at the beginning, during that entire time, I was going through a divorce at the same time of assuming office. Divorce can be devastating to some people. One can suffer from depression, but I believe because I kept myself busy with board meetings, four children and attending College of the Desert part time, I didn't allow these feelings to overcome me. I just simply didn't have the time for them. My children and now newly adopted children (18,000 to be exact) was my impulse to continue being positive at all times.

I believe I am here in this position for the right reasons: to provide quality programs to our children, to provide safer schools, and to provide the right resources and materials for our children. The number of Board Members in the Coachella Valley District is a total of seven. Can you imagine getting seven different heads agreeing on things? I can honestly say in our recent votes, 99 percent have been unanimous. I feel so grateful to be part of this team. I wouldn't change anything in the world. I am eagerly looking forward to many positive changes in our Coachella Valley Unified School District.

About the Author

Yolanda Castro is a single mother of four who was raised in Michoacan, MX by her grandparents Maria and Alfonso. She was born in Indio, CA. She has been an active parent volunteer for ten years in Coachella District. She is currently attending college and sitting as a Board Member in the Coachella Valley Unified School District.

The People Who Keep Me Up at Night

Marissa Davisson

"We are unusual and tragic and alive."

~Dave Eggers

A Heartbreaking Work of Staggering Genius

As I'm lying in bed, my door begins to creak. I watch it slowly open; the hall light dances on my face as I look to see who was pushing in the door. It continues to make an awful noise. My mind races. It feels like eternity, but finally the hall light beams around a dark figure. I still can't identify the culprit.

"Dad?"

The door slammed shut before the entire word even made it out of my mouth. The waves of fear crash against me; I am being swept up, and I'm tumbling through the sea foam as my breath is being stolen and my eyes forced open. I pull the cool sheets over my face praying this feeling of dread dies down. I start to feel my hot, wet breath building up. My world begins to spin; I can't move too fast, or I'll fall flat on my face. The spinning is getting faster and faster.

Who am I seeing? Why are they here? Will they ever leave me alone?

I can't take this anymore. I fling the sheets off of me with my hands and feet. I lie flat on my back, welcoming the small goose bumps forming on my cooling skin.

I saw this figure of a man throughout my childhood, but since my dad died I like to think it is him. Although there is likely no connection between the two, imagining my dad checking up on me feels a lot better than some strange creature stalking me in the night.

I let out a sigh, and the spinning starts to slow. I sit on the edge of my bed with my feet dangling right above the floor. I push my palms against my closed eyelids and start to pray for forgiveness. I must have done something atrocious to have these people follow me.

I begin to mutter, "Please Lord, forgive me of my sins. I will follow you more closely. I want to be used by you. Help me to be better and do better. Send these spirits away, Lord. Leave me with..."

I'm interrupted with the pitter-patter of tiny feet against the wood floors. *No, not again.* Tears sting as they flow from my tired eyes. They're here. It's been six months; a new town, new house, and new prescriptions, yet they're still here. The children never seem to leave me be.

I hear the little fists knock upon my door. I can't do this tonight. I'm sick of being tired. The tears continue to stream down my face; I watch them splatter against my bare thighs. I hear another knock and a small giggle mimicking an old, pull-string doll. The hall light is showing the two sets of feet resting behind my closed door. I can't do this anymore. I need to escape. This anger is welling up inside of me. The knocking starts again, but this time they do not stop. It goes on and on and on.

I'm done. I jump from my bed and run for my door. I swing it open in a fury, and in an instant, the light flips off, and I hear them running down the hall away from me. I cannot see them; I can only hear them. I scream out of anguish. I slam the door with everything I have in me.

As I start walking back to my bed, I contemplate if I would have done anything if had I opened the door and the two children would have been standing there, looking straight at me. I'm sure I would have frozen, but I want to see them. I don't want to follow them, but I want to see their faces. I want to know who they are.

My face hits the pillow, and I start to think about Jack. He never thought I was insane, just abnormal. I explained my susceptibility and closeness with this other world to him. I told him about the things I saw, felt, and heard. In those moments, he made me feel comfortable in my skin and, in some senses, normal. He even told me that he once heard that these entities, he loved to use that word, that many people see are categorized as such: the men are here to help you now, the women help you in the future, and children deceive you. But this seems so backwards; how could the kids be the deceptive ones?

I wish he could remember where he heard about all that. I want to spill my guts to someone who knows, who sees, who agrees it isn't all in my head. I could never contact anyone without being anonymous. My fear of institutionalization outweighs my curiosity. I can't be locked away. I have horrifying nightmares of scraping my bleeding, bent fingers down the concrete walls of a makeshift prison. I wake up gasping for air.

Jack used to tell me to see a psychic, but I will never do that. I cannot dabble in the spirit world. I don't want to commune with the dead; I actually want to stop hearing the input of the crowd in my home. I'm tired of running from my own thoughts. If I'm being completely honest, I also constantly struggle with what others think of me. I know the people I once loved and trusted look at me with pity and a little fear. They don't even know the whole story – they are believing what they want to, which is, most likely, that I'm just insane. Sometimes, I start to believe I'm just crazy, especially since Jack left me. He kept me grounded. Now, I'm struggling to hold myself down. But if the medication doesn't stop them from coming, it mustn't be a mental illness, meaning they are actually here – or, that I am just so insane that I believe that.

Turning to lay on my back, I start to list all the reasons why I am not crazy. Months ago, Jack and I were lounging on the couch, and we heard a crash in the kitchen; I sent him in. He came back with a pan in hand and began to laugh, "It just fell from the lower cabinet." I smiled, hiding a little disappointment. I was hoping he'd see one of them; he said he believed me, but I wanted him to see them himself; I believe he wanted to see them too. I felt he needed reassurance in my sanity.

The knocking begins again.

I reach for a bottle on my nightstand. I overestimate the distance of the bottles and create a cloud clank and send one down, crashing on the floor.

"Damn it!"

I turn the bedroom light on to see the damage. The tinted green glass shattered everywhere. The knocking is getting louder and more frequent now. I turn to face the door, and I see the small feet have been replaced with one large pair.

I whispered, "Who's there?"

The hall light switches off again. But then it happened, the moment I have been waiting for: I heard him talk. He grumbles, "I'm here to talk."

My heart misses a beat, and I cannot find my words. I have been playing out this moment in my head for years and planned exactly what I would say, but now all that collected information is gone. I am lost without words. Then, he speaks again, "Can I come in?"

I want to scream things like *No, leave me alone* or *Never come here again.* But I do not; before I can stop my mouth from uttering the words, I reply, "Yes." In an instant, the tall and frail man with a fedora placed aslant comes waltzing in. The lights dim as he walks towards me. Out of shock, I take a step back and step on a few shards of glass.

Without taking my eyes off of him, I sit back down on my bed. The stinging in my heel causes me to look down at it. As I look away from the man, piercing pain starts in my temples and makes my world spin again. I pull my legs in towards me as I rock on the edge of the bed. The blood is dripping down the side of my crisp, white sheets now. The room is spinning faster and faster. I'm holding my eyes shut. I can't hear anything but a low hum. I'm trying to hold on – I don't want to throw up. I'm rocking back and forth violently.

The man kneels beside my bed. He swoops me up and holds me like a baby. I wrap my aching arms around him and take a deep breath into his ill-fitting suit jacket. I start to wail like a child. This closeness has been missing from my life for so long. Then, he lays me down softly. He places me on my side, facing away from him and the door. I can feel him lean in close to me. He starts to whisper softly in my ear. I can no longer make out his words. I just feel a soft tickle of his unkempt facial hair and warm breath against me. I start to feel like I'm sinking into my bed. I want to rearrange my body, but I cannot muster the energy. My eyes feel so heavy. I try to wrap my head around everything, and I just can't get a grip. I can no longer hold my eyes open, so I decide to abandon consciousness. I drift away.

Then, the banging starts again. The sunlight is cracking through the drawn shades. I turn my weak body towards the door. It's the children again. The knocking is so loud and intense I can feel it in my temples; the sides of my head are pounding with the perpetual knocking. I scope the room for the man. I had hoped he was lying beside me in bed, but he is not. I'm lying here completely alone with these children banging on my door. This sums up my existence – my sad, pathetic existence. I am tired, alone, and yet, not alone. It sounds like I'm talking about aliens or something. Who knows? They could be aliens running some tests on human mental strength. Whatever they are is foreign to me.

I'm so done with this existence. I want out. I want to escape. I can't hold onto my sanity any longer. I have nothing to live for, nothing to strive for. My nightlife tears apart any hope of normality or success. I cannot be or do anything. I wish I could sleep forever.

I want them to be real; I want the man to be mine or to leave me forever. I never want to hear the children laugh again. I want to give into this darkness building in me. Every day is a struggle that I no longer have any fight for. I'm giving in.

I grab a long piece of green glass from the floor. Lying back down, I look up at it. I see a droplet of wet blood twinkle in the hall light. This is it. I am leaving this world for good.

I hold my left arm up straight towards the ceiling and dig the glass from my palm up through my forearm. I watch the beautiful red blood rush down my arm and then, over my chest. I tilt my head towards the door and watch it flow down the side of the bed. I imagine it creating a puddle around me. I watch myself swim in it. My mind is flickering from blood to black and then, back to blood.

I hear a long, hissing noise. I think it may be a voice. I can't quite make it out. I can tell it's a woman. *Is she talking to me?* I slur, "Hello." I try to sit up to get a better picture of what's occurring in my room. My head is spinning once again, but in such a new way. I see the bright screen of my cell phone on my floor. *Who's talking on my phone?* I try to find my feet on the floor, but I wind up flinging myself down. Lying on my stomach, I can see that my hand is just inches from the phone. I'm losing strength, but I need to know who is talking. I use all my energy to move my hand to the phone. I hear the groggy voice say, "Help is on its way." I try to muster up a *No, I'm fine*. But I cannot get a word out – I'm fading. Everything is becoming a blur. I feel myself sinking into the floor.

I start to see a piercing light through my eyelids. My eyes hurt, but I manage to pry them open. Everything around me is bright and foggy. It feels calm; I'm at peace. I am free. I close my eyes and try to slip away again. I breathe deep and exhale slowly.

Then, I hear a thump. I open my eyes quickly. My hearts sinks. I open my eyes again, but this time I'm in a hospital room. I lived – Unfortunately, I lived. I have to do this all over again. I cannot do it. I am broken and weak. I start to cry hysterically. Tears stream down my face, tickling my cheek. I go to sweep them away with my fingers and realize my arms are strapped down to the bed. I try to break free, flinging my limbs every way possible. A crowd of medical staff comes racing in my room. The blonde nurse in blue Garfield scrubs says, "Calm down. You had an accident."

All the people in the room have their hands on me – nurses are holding my hands, doctors injecting substances, orderlies forcing my legs straight. I'm up against an entire hospital. "I just want my hands free," I scream. The Garfield nurse squawks, "We can't do that. You're a danger to yourself and others." I cannot do anything, but thrash and scream. I look down the bed to count the useless people in my room and notice the blood coming through my arm's bandage. I feel the sinking feeling again. My eyes are closing against my will. I'm trying to stay conscious, but I'm drifting away. *How could this have happened?*

I finally wake again, but this time the room is dark. I see a lit lamp on the nightstand beside me. This soft, yellow light is comforting. I feel the tightened straps on my wrists and ankles. I try to remain calm with a deep breath and a prayer.

But a knock interrupts my mumbled words. I do not say

anything – I just lie still, praying for a family member, or even the Garfield nurse, to walk through the door. But my prayers went unanswered. He came walking in, but this time with his fedora pressed up against his chest exposing is balding head. I start to weep.

This is my life. I couldn't even end it. I am forced to converse with the unknown. The weeping turns to sobbing. I have given up. He wraps his fingers around my toes and squeezes them tight. He then drags his fingertips from the bottom of my foot, up my legs, up my stomach, between my breasts, and up to my neck. Then, he tilts my head up and whispers, "Chin up. It ain't all that bad."

About the Author

Marissa Davisson is an esthetician and student in Fullerton, California. She enjoys her time with her three-year-old son, Charlie, taking Disneyland trips, and cake decorating. Being one of four daughters, she is surrounded by family. She hopes to see the world one day, especially the countries of Africa. When it comes to writing, Marissa likes to write about supernatural happenings and the mis-adventures of everyday life.

Marissa finds the most challenging part of writing to be getting the ideas from her mind onto paper. She looks forward to cultivating her writing skills and studying many subjects in school. Although this is Marissa's first time publishing her writing, she plans to compose and publish at least a couple more short stories.

Walk to the Store

Kimberly Enriquez

My name is Crystal Page. I am twelve years old. I was abducted at the age of ten in the year 1983, in a small town called Preston. Its population is consistently around five thousand. I was a young joyous girl with brown wavy locks, blue eyes as clear as the sea, skin white as snow, and freckles that ran across my cheekbones and forehead. I was always the type of child to run around and play ball outside in the hottest, sunniest or coldest, freezing, winters. I mostly played football with the boys instead of playing volleyball with the girls like I should have been. I loved to compete, and I didn't mind a nudge here and there. I wasn't afraid of the weather, sports, or boys. I wasn't afraid of anything.

Every afternoon, I would go to the lofty market for a little stroll to buy some of my favorite junk food, which included rainbow Skittles, hot Cheetos, and ice cold Coca Cola. My parents always permitted me go to the store on my own. It was at the corner of the block. They thought because it was so close nothing could ever happen to me; plus, I never wandered off. But as I didn't know and they didn't know, someone had been watching me for the last two weeks.

He would watch me during the times I would play outside and the times I would go to the lofty market. He calculated and planned everything to avoid getting caught. To be more specific, he found a way to reel me in. I knew who this man was; he was no stranger to me. It was my neighbor forty-two year old Don Jefferson. He lived across the street from us, just a few houses down. I would rarely see him outside. The only times I did see him was when he would trim or water his plants and perhaps pick up his mail.

Don wasn't the type of person you would see caroling on Christmas or handing out candy on Halloween. He always kept to himself. He was always quite odd. He had short brown hair that never grew out, and he dressed with casual faded jeans, a long sleeve shirt and a knit sweater. He wore the same style as always, no matter how the weather was. It was his signature look. Little did I know, this man would be the one take to my childhood, joy and air.

I was headed to the store on one hot windy afternoon when the red horizon had hit earth and the sky had pasted its mood. The air was crisp and hot, blowing my hair to the sides. No cars were heard, not even a bird's simplest chirp. Only my lazy steps were heard dragging across the pavement floor. I remember I felt uneasy that day with every step I took the closer I got to the store. I had asked myself why did I feel so melancholy. Maybe I just needed my junk food to cheer me up. That always got me into a good mood.

I walked a few more steps, and I was there at the lofty market. I got my junk food, greeted the clerk lady Jessy as always, and paid. Then, I was on my way home. However, as I walked out, something unfamiliar happened. My neighbor Don was outside the store. I flashed him my white bright smile and continued to walk home. But as I was walking, he walked by my side. I was on the sidewalk, and he was at the edge of the road. He didn't seem mind and started to converse.

Don made quick but fascinating talk about these new born three-month-old brown Labrador puppies his sister had given him for his birthday. He wanted me to see them, but I knew it wasn't the right time, and I had to head home. However, he kept bragging about how cute, tiny, and fluffy they were. He said he was thinking of giving me one as well. He figured since I was his neighbor, he might as well give me one because he didn't want all those puppies to himself. I thought about it a while and decided what the heck I might as well see them. They were just puppies; my parents would understand. I was really anxious to see the Labrador puppies. I couldn't help but smile at the mention of him wanting to give me one to. I am a big animal lover. I had three cats, three dogs, eight chickens, and a hamster. I couldn't doubt that he knew that too.

He then convinced me with the nonstop detail of the puppies. I couldn't resist any longer. At that point in the conversation, he had asked me once again if I wanted to go see them. I nodded my head in agreement. As we crossed the empty street, I looked up curiously at him and noticed he had a weird crooked smile running across his chapped lips. I just thought perhaps he didn't have the best smile, but he was trying to be friendly. Who would have known within a few minutes I would know his true intentions and reality would hit me hard in the face.

He opened the door for me. As I walked in, a strong smell of cigarettes and bacon brushed against my nose. It was a smell I wasn't familiar with. My house always smelled like fresh roses or women's perfume. I walked further into the house. It was pretty neat and organized. Picture frames hanged against the walls, furniture at its place, and there was a new wood floor, as it seemed. Besides the smell of the cigarettes, the house seemed fine, just like any other American house. Strangely, I didn't hear any whimpers, smell or any view of the puppies.

Then, I turned and asked him confusingly, "Sir, where are the puppies?" He looked down at me and flashed his crooked smile again and said, "Dear, there were no puppies in the first place."

At first, my mind didn't recollect what he had just told me. My head was spinning. I didn't understand what was going on or what was going to happen to me. But as my world started spinning, he began to walk towards me. I tried to run, but I stumbled and fell hopelessly against the wooden floor. He picked me up and started walking down to the basement. As he walked steadily down the stairs, he caressed my face. I kicked and screamed and even tried punching him, but nobody could have heard my desperate cries, and I knew it too well after every lower step he too to the basement. I had no idea how I was going to get out of there.

As I frantically tried to scramble out of his arms, he looked and me and said, "You're mine." I cried and cried. I couldn't stop. Then, we had finally made it to the shadowed dark basement. That afternoon, my innocence was taken away.

It has been two sad long years that I have been locked up in his basement. I don't understand how they didn't see Don as a possible suspect. I spent sunrise after sunrise and shining moonlight after moonlight there. Every single one of them I had missed because of this dreadful dark basement.

I wonder everyday how my family is doing or what they think has happened to me. Do they think I died, ran away or disappeared? If only they knew that I am still here. Their baby girl is hanging on and waiting for them to find her. I never give up hope for the day I get out of this jail of a basement to once again feel the hot sun's heat soaking into my pores and to be able to see the moonlight and its little brothers and sisters the stars and to once again run and play ball in the streets in the winter days.

I never give up hope. I never will. How am I? Crystal Page...

About the Author

Kimberly Enriquez is nineteen years old and a freshman at College of the Desert. She tends to persuade the major of Psychology. She lives in a small town called Salton City and lives three miles away from the lake. Sometimes, she likes to walk around there for a peaceful and tranquil time, with just herself, the lake, and the air.

In her free time, she loves to watch movies or just sit in her room and listen to music. She's a calm girl, who doesn't go out, and she really can't go out because Salton City is a small place where there isn't much to do. There's only desert and the lake, but that's the beauty of it. There's no noise or disturbances.

Changing Tides

Raena Fisk

Escape

The sun shines down on the vineyards
Another day
Grapes are pungent in the heat
Like a wet dog in summer
The valley is beautiful
But I've been here too long
It's time to more on
Visit new places
See unfamiliar faces
Just for one day

~Raena Fisk

Looking up, I see the waning gibbous moon illuminating the sand. Picking up a palm full reveals that it's damp and holds together well. I try to sit and shield myself from the biting wind blowing off the top of my sand dune and succeed, reminding myself of the same wind that whips across my face when I ride my bike to school in the morning. Behind me, the Pacific Ocean roars. I am completely and utterly alone.

I remember my first road trip to Dillon Beach, California. It was almost nine years ago, when I was young enough to still think I knew everything about the world. At the time, it was my kingdom, and I was the queen of it all, from Tomales Point to the northern tip of Bodega Bay. It was a place of happiness and serenity, and as I got older, it became the place where I went to leave my hectic world of reality behind to escape to the freedom of the sea and salt. This time, however, my feeling of ecstasy is heavily tainted with a sense of loss, or that something (or someone) is missing. It's ironic, seeing how I always come out here to feel complete.

Another gust of wind slaps me in the face, and I decide to move away from the choppy airspace at the top of the dune. Walking down to the pebbly beach, I wonder why I chose to come here at this time of day, or rather, night. But then again, I think to myself, it's worth it just to be out here once more.

Continuing up the shore, I stagger slightly from the wind and yearn to be inside the little cafe at the entrance to the small beach town that is Dillon Beach, with a gigantic mug of their incomparable hot chocolate. My hood refuses to cooperate and keeps being blown off my head. The tiny flashlight in my mouth is my only beacon, but I turn it off and let the moonlight guide me. This entire time I am unable to think of anything but the cold. Combined with the shadows of the cliffs and jagged rocks that line the surf, it makes me think that something is watching me, that my demons have tracked me here. I'm confused as to why this place is giving me these feelings of unease. Why has my childhood safe haven morphed into such a hostile environment?

My footsteps crumble the sand beneath me, as if to mock my attempt to depart from civilization and lay down a bright, shining path for my demons to follow. The jagged slab of granite I now sit on reminds me of said demons, Unease and Crisis, along with their daughter Sorrow. Unwanted recollections are forced to the front of my mind: a prank gone horribly wrong, a friendship torn apart, and a year of painful regret.

I now remember why I haven't come back in so many months. A scene begins to unfold before my eyes, taking shape and reality as a whip-like strand of brown seaweed flashes in front of me. An unmistakable *crack* reverberates inside my skull. A young girl screams and drops to her knees before me, her hands over her face as her fingers begin to leak, a trickle of rust at first but quickly becoming a deep, rich crimson. I observe her, confused by her anguish, until I look down at my own hands to see the tool of her despair resting in my palm. The scene swirls, obscured by my unconscious trying to block it out completely but not before my own wail of realization echoes through my mind. I shake my head.

Is there no end to the violence? I have no choice but to carry on off the rock and up the beach, searching for some point of relief while getting nothing but another smack of airborne ice to my features and fingers. My extremities are numb. My mind is clogged with harsh thoughts of the past. My once great kingdom has turned to evil and despair.

My haven has become a frigid hell.

I look for an escape, some bush or boulder that can spare me from this cold, bitter land. I journey onward, willing myself to keep going and persevere. Now with each slap from the gusts of wind comes a distinct and strong scent of salt and brine. I continue walking, dodging the surges of the incoming tide, until I come to a graveyard of giant boulders and cliff points. It is my final destination, and my reason for slugging through the desolate waste that was once my oceanside empire.

I start on the south end, knowing that the object I search for is there. My flashlight beams over every stone and pebble in vain, as it reveals nothing. I search the north end as well despite my logical judgment, taking an extremely close look at every rock that could possibly be the one, but come up with nothing. Accepting defeat, I turn back down the beach, only to spot a most familiar shape in front of me.

My serpentine. Or rather, my father's, for he has always said that he'd relocate it to our front yard someday. There it is, all two tons of it, its emerald sheen reflecting the moonlight in between its milky white streaks of quartz. The serpentine boulder was once a decorative piece in the backyard of one of the houses on the cliffs above me but had long since fallen to sea level when the cliff had eroded away. It's a familiar figure, a constant, ever-present entity that I always visit out here. The sight of it brings me relief, for not all in my kingdom has changed.

Suddenly, the beach calls a truce. The hostility ends. The wind is nothing but a salty breeze to me now. The sea is a sleepy but joyful hum of peace, and I have literally found my rock.

I hear a car horn in the distance. Quickly, I pat the rock that has become such a part of me as the beach has and turn back to walk the way I came. As I reach the foot of the path to the small grove of pine bushes that was once my castle's fortress, I race up the hill to the top, where the little house that served as my castle is perched. I walk off the sandy slope of the hill onto the asphalt dead-end at the top and see my father's convertible sitting in front of the house. The engine starts up as I walk to the passenger's side door. A final glance toward the horizon impresses a sinister sight.

The pine bushes sway scarily in the wind. The ocean roars mightily and out of sight. The clouds on the horizon are shadowy and looming in the moonlight. The silhouettes of the cliffs stretch across the sand and throw everything else into a menacing darkness, a field of unknowing.

It is terrifying, but it is my kingdom…

My haven…   My home.

About the Author

Born and raised in the heart of Wine Country (a.k.a. Napa, California), Raena Fisk began writing poetry at the age of fourteen, which inspired her to eventually try her hand at short stories and essays. Along with writing, her hobbies include making frequent trips to the beach, trying new foods, cosplaying, singing, and video games. Her family and friendships are what she holds most dear, and she considers her greatest achievement to date to be her bilinguality in English and Spanish. She is currently pursuing a degree in Journalism at Fullerton College, in Fullerton, CA.

Morning Sun

Sandra Flores

It was 3:07am on a Friday, in Seattle. Sarah looked at the wooden desk clock near her bed in a state of confusion and sadness, exclusively felt during the early morning hours. She had just moved away from her mother's home in Brooklyn a few weeks prior and decided to head back to the city of her birth, despite it being a city she barely even knew. A few days ago, she received a letter from her best friend Noelle, who was currently attending art school in Chicago and over the course of three years had become unattached and aloof with Sarah. Sarah's undying loyalty and admiration for her was put to a halt when Noelle came to a decision to distance herself.

Sarah felt abandoned and spiteful, yet she still clung onto the hope that their friendship was still there, temporarily hidden by an eclipse. As adolescence came to its expected end, Noelle secretly decided to temporarily sever ties with Sarah. She had convinced herself that if she were to linger over her past, she wouldn't be fully prepared for the future she always wanted. In Noelle's eyes, Sarah was a pulsating, oozing wound. Noelle knew that with each wound comes a bandage, and when the time comes to remove a bandage, it must be with care and precision, which is how Noelle decided to leave behind Sarah.

Over time, her trust in Noelle diminished. She felt she was holding onto a fictitious friendship, as if Noelle had never existed. This all contributed to Sarah's departure from her mother's home in Brooklyn. As much as she wanted to take the blame for leaving home, it was Noelle's life that inspired her to leave and find her own. It was her free-spirit that showed her there was more to life than just living. Noelle was born with an identity and a soul so luminescent and artful. Sarah began an endeavor to nourish her own.

The letter was unexpected and out of character. Sarah began to wonder how Noelle got a hold of her new address and why she even bothered writing a letter in this day in age. She was then hit by a wave of old emotions. She felt her emptiness and dependence on Noelle resurface within seconds. She tried to remind herself that a true best friend wouldn't forget about her, but none of that seemed to work. She reread the letter over and over again. Her eyes grew weary and began to burn with each blink, yet she still continued to whisper the words inaudibly. It was pouring outside, and as much as she hated realizing it, the bitter winter storms knew their way around the city better than she did. Before folding the letter in half, she read a line one last time, "*Sarah, I hope you're well, and I hope you cope with change.*"

Anger rushed through her veins like a drug as she crumpled the letter and threw it on the floor. She fell asleep as the rain began to stop. The city streets were empty and the lights reflected off of the wet roads like a dirty mirror. For a moment, everything was still and nothing in her world was alive. Her pulse was faint, the outside world felt dead, everything that was beautiful and everything that was hideous ceased to exist the second she gave up control of her thoughts. Everything went with her: the good and the bad.

Her sleep was brief, and Sarah found herself staring through the nothingness of darkness. The darkness bluntly forced her to face her thoughts. She hated remembering. She tasted the bitterness in her mouth and felt resentment deep within herself. There was no one to blame. She couldn't blame God, her mother, the universe, not even Noelle. The fault couldn't fall onto a particular thing or person or entity, but it felt as if it were everywhere, even when it belonged to no one.

It wasn't Noelle's fault that she couldn't handle their friendship anymore. She never expected or wanted Noelle to feel the need to understand her. She just had no one else to watch her unfold emotions for what they really were. She thought about her father again, and she tried to distract herself with her animosity towards Noelle. She was hurt Noelle brought up her father's death in the letter as if it were a simple incident she could erase from her life. It all came rushing back to her as a hurricane of buried recollections.

Sarah's father died when she was five years old in a violent car crash on a busy street in Paris, just a few months before Princess Diana met a similar fate in the same city. That morning, she distinctly remembered waking up with the sun in her face, something that she never experienced beforehand, and she thought it was pure luck. Never did it cross her mind that eight hours later someone would phone her mother and explain the tragedy that unfolded on a busy Parisian street.

Two hours after the phone call, the sobbing, the screaming, and the hysterics that escaped from her mother's mouth, they boarded on a train from their expat home in London, England, to the city where her father took his last breath in a small yellow cab. The train ride was eternal. Sarah didn't necessarily remember the words her mother used to tell her she was never going to see her father again. She remembers the deeply troubled look in her mother's eyes, the midnight-black river of mascara-stained tears streaming down her face, and her aging skin and lips forming a frown so vile and sad. That stayed with Sarah more than any string of words she ever heard.

After her father's burial in London, she and her mother left their home in England and flew back to the States where Sarah had not been since she was born in Seattle. They settled in a roach-infested apartment in Brooklyn where her mother became a preschool teacher and taught Sarah how to paint as a form of free therapy. She continued on with her life and made a bundle of friends, including Noelle.

As they got older, Noelle would come to realize Sarah would hold everything in until she felt as if she couldn't hold the words inside any longer. She would refrain from speaking about her genuine sentiments until the words parted her lips and forcefully crawled out of her mouth like little spiders. Despite this, Sarah never cared much for her words or anyone else's words. What intrigued her most was the roaring thunder of what felt like excitement, grief, and loneliness that would form together to create something she couldn't fully express with words. She would try to explain the sudden spell of cryptic energy to Noelle, but she would fail miserably. She felt this surge the most when she thought about her father and the very few vague memories she still had of him. Noelle believed Sarah had never gotten over his death and tried to help her fulfill what she needed to complete herself. Sarah refused her help and preferred sulking within, unknowingly pushing Noelle away.

Sarah thought about their friendship before it accumulated cuts and bruises, before Sarah selfishly assumed Noelle picked herself over their friendship, before Sarah was angry and isolated, and before Sarah came face to face with her own selfishness. She felt a strange, faint peace rise over her, and she began to write a response to Noelle's unannounced letter from a cloudless perspective:

I'm petty, jealous, selfish, and prone to self-aggrandizement by nature, and I am sorry. Your friendship makes me feel more appreciative of human life and human connections, like when I witnessed the mailman and my neighbor talking about their favorite baseball teams and seeing the faint glow in their eyes and hearing the excitement in their voices when they said their goodbyes. I thought of us. I look forward to talking to you and hearing your stories because for a few seconds I live through your words. I know you don't share certain moments of your life, and neither do I at times, but despite that I feel as if our connection and friendship is genuine and we can put the pieces together without any hints as to where they go. This deep-rooted connection may end up dying along with us, but I wouldn't kill it even if it asked me to. I want to be able to say that I saw it until it was over, until our friendship felt its last sudden rush of adrenaline.

That's when Sarah felt her own words under her skin and implanted in her brain. She felt alive again. She felt the morning sun on her face. It was the purest of luck.

About the Author

Sandra Flores is a seventeen-year-old college student from Southern California. She occasionally writes for an online zine called Pop Culture Puke and occasionally writes just for herself in a moleskin notebook. She enjoys walking around Los Angeles, making art, and spending too much time on social media.

Riley's Garden

Caroline Foster

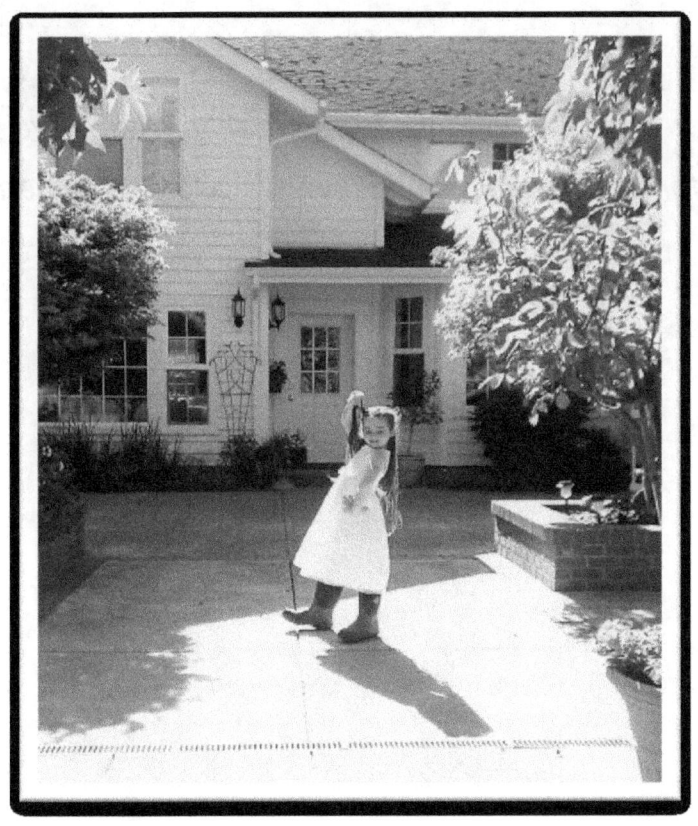

"Children do live in fantasy and reality; they move back and forth very easily in a way we no longer remember how to do."

~Maurice Sendak

On one hot, sunny day, there was a humble little girl who had just turned seven. She had long blonde hair with crystal blue eyes that would melt anyone's heart. Her name was Riley, and she loved to be outside. She loved the feeling of the warm, rocky gravel under her feet and the cool breeze going through her Rapunzel hair. She almost never wore any shoes. Riley was in love with the Earth; she did everything she could do to make sure she was doing her part. Since Riley had so much passion and love for the Earth, she grew her own garden. She was growing luscious purple, rosy pink, and golden yellow tulips. Also, she grew vegetables, such as juicy olive green cucumber, butternut squash, and bright red chili peppers.

Every day, Riley would go outside and look at her garden to make sure the vegetables were growing healthily. On the days she had school, she would rush home to check on her lovely plants. Sometimes, she would even speak to her plants as if they could hear her. She would talk about her days at school or anything she wanted to talk about.

Every night, Riley made sure she watered her plants and said goodnight before she went to bed. As Riley crawled into bed, she would sometimes wish her plants would talk back to her. Then that night, something amazing happened! There was a rush of bright shooting stars shooting from one end of the sky then flew into disappearance into the dark mysterious night sky. As soon as she saw the star, Riley immediately wished her plants would talk back to her. Before she finished the wish, one of the stars landed right in her garden. Riley couldn't believe what she saw. It was as if she had seen a ghost. So with much excitement, she quickly ran out her room and went straight to her garden. The star had broken into thousands of pieces, making a cloud of dust that covered her entire garden. In awe, Riley couldn't decide if she was dreaming, so she lay down hoping the plants would start talking, and soon, she fell asleep.

The next morning, Riley woke up in her bed and wondered if it was a dream. She went outside to check on her garden and everything looked normal, as if nothing happened. While she was walking away in disappointment, she stumbled across a sparkly glow over her bright red chili peppers. She wasn't sure what was going on with her garden or why the pepper was glowing. She realized the shooting star did happen, and she was not dreaming. Riley hovered over the glowing pepper with her face lit up like a red balloon. It was as if she was staring at a broken stoplight. She sat there and started to talk to the pepper, yet there were no response, except for the flashing glow the pepper gave off.

Riley then became disappointed again and walked in the house to get ready for school. Once she arrived at school, she began to tell all her friends what happened, but no one seemed to believe her. All the kids laughed, mocked, and teased her. She told them to come look at the pepper themselves if they didn't believe her.

After school, none of the kids showed up, so she went on with her normal routine of watering and taking care of her garden. When she came across the peppers, the bright red one was still glowing. She walked over and stood beside it, waiting for something to happen. As she was about to walk away, the pepper started to move, but she did not notice it. She went inside to eat dinner and told her parents about her day. Her dad told her, "Ignore the kids, honey, but making up white lies is not right." Riley became upset because no one seemed to believe her about the shooting star.

After dinner, Riley did not want to go back outside to check on the pepper because of what her father mentioned. She was sad and perfect droplets of tears started to fall from her rosy freckled, chubby cheeks. Her mom walked in to say goodnight and noticed Riley was upset. She gave Riley the biggest and warmest hug a mother could give to make all her problems go away. She told her to get some sleep and everything would be better in the morning.

The next morning, Riley felt better and went about her day in her garden like the usual happy Riley before everything happened. Like every morning, she checked every plant to see how they were doing. She walked over to the peppers, and surprisingly, the same one was still flashing. It said, "Well, good morning, Riley!" Excitedly, Riley jumped as high as she could into the air full with joy. She could not retain her excitement, so she picked up the pepper and began to dance and sway away through her garden. Riley knew all along she was not lying and everything was true.

She began telling the pepper her stories and problems, and she received nothing but the best response back. The pepper said, "I will always be here if you need a friend or anyone to talk to." All of a sudden, a rush of happy tears burst from Riley's big blue eyes. She thanked the pepper with so much joy and happiness for being a friend to her. All Riley ever wanted was a friend, even if it were a vegetable. She was still the same humble little girl who loved the earth and her garden.

About the Author

Caroline Foster graduated from Palm Springs High School in 2014. Caroline never found much inspiration in writing until she entered college. She wishes to pursue a career in writing children's books. Her true career is to be a registered nurse at St. Jude's.

At Least I've Got You, Winston

Alexander D. Francisco

"In every walk with nature,
one receives far more than he seeks."

~John Muir

I hate Mondays. But maybe today is Tuesday or Wednesday. I've honestly got no clue. I found later it was a Sunday all along.

It's the end of spring. I'm sitting here on a rock placed at the junction of two hiking trails in western Virginia. *At least I'm not in West Virginia,* I laughed to myself. This is the most beautiful piece of the earth as far as I'm concerned. I'm on a bald peak, looking into a nameless valley; the spruces and the firs do not dot the slopes but rather blanket them entirely. That vividness of green stays with you. On either side of the bald is an entrance back into the mystery, into the dense forests of Appalachia. In this clearing, the narrow and winding trail is flanked by a knee-high brown grass that no one ever cared to identify to a hiker ignorant of the flora and fauna before he ventured out here.

But I'm fucking hungry! I've got no way to tell time, but based on the sun and my stomach, it's lunchtime. When you've been eating between 4 and 6,000 calories a day, no food by lunch is uncomfortable. On this 80-mile leg of the hike, I've run out of food. Now, the situation may be serious, but not life-threatening. Today is day four in between towns, and, therefore, resupply points. I thought I was going to be done in four days, but one lazy day was followed by a rainy day, and before you know it you've got wet boots, no food, and twenty-two more miles to a Chinese buffet. I honestly felt I *needed* some Chinese. A Los Angelino can only eat fried chicken and drink Pabst Blue Ribbon for so long before he craves something a little more diverse. We're so spoiled.

How the hell did I get here? Let's flashback for a moment: I came out here three months ago with two friends from high school, ready to conquer the most famous of long-distance backpacking trails: The Appalachian Trail. With absolutely no experience, gear, mental preparedness for backpacking, but with ample need for adventure and an excuse to get out of my dead-end job, I dove in wholeheartedly. The 2,200 mile behemoth snakes her way from Georgia to Maine, and we were around mile 500 when I decided to take a break from my comrades for a few days. I was told that after that long in the middle of nowhere with anyone, you either fall in love with the people you're with, or you think you start to think about killing them. I was experiencing the latter.

This is why I'm alone on this bald peak.

Well, I guess I'm not entirely alone…

"At least I've got you, Winston."

Yes Winston, as in Winston Red cigarettes, manufactured and produced by the R.J Reynolds Tobacco Company in b-e-a-utiful Winston-Salem, North Carolina.

Now, for those of you who don't smoke, quit smoking, or are assaulted by memories of an overbearing babysitter or cheek-pinching grandmother, words like "poison," "cancer," "noxious," and "death" may come to mind.

But for those who do smoke, you know what I'm talking about. Because when you light that sucker up and take the first long, full draw, hold the smoke in your lungs for just a moment, you tilt your head back, exhale the light gray smoke, and you realize that life isn't so bad anymore. No one's got any problems for the first half of a cigarette.

So, I begin to rummage through my large pack, trying to find the only piece of equipment I *must* keep dry. Yes, the smokes. From a Ziplock sandwich bag I pull out the pack, whittled down to less than half of its capacity the last couple of days. The red and white box is covered in labels about the ill-effects, warnings that are never read. And in a slightly italicized serif font in huge red letters, it says *Winston.* The text wraps around the box, so on the front face only *Win* is displayed, as if I have something to gain, some sort of prize inside.

Now where's my lighter?

"Goddamnit!" I said the expletive out loud.

One of my hiking mates has my lighter.

But, maybe I've got those matches in here. This is definitely a longshot, but maybe, just maybe, that book I put in here weeks ago has found its way down to a safe place.

"Yes," I whisper, and I pull out the thin book of matches, hiding underneath -

One wet match...

Well, a lot of fucking good that does me.

Admitting defeat, I re-pack my things and move along the trail again. I take solace in the fact that today is the most lovely we've had in a week. The sun is out, and the sky is cloudless. This means that the humidity is at least tolerable. Have you ever been to the South in the summer? It's like wearing a wet fur coat in a sauna; it's the kind of humidity where you sweat while sticking your head out of the water during a swim in a *crick* (not "creek," mind you. Crick).

I'm back in the forest again. The air is cool and still. Not even a breeze comes through the dense trees, and my mind begins to wonder, as it does when hiking for hours and hours alone.

The night before, I was having a few ounces of whiskey and another, another, another cigarette before bed. A guy was sitting there with an acoustic guitar across his lap, playing songs he loved and missed. But if you told me that the only song he knew was "Where is My Mind," by the Pixies, I would have believed it.

This is the fourth time he played it, I realized. *He must be from Boston... Or he's filled with angst.*

He suddenly interrupted himself. "This trip, this hike - it has to be about you. It can't be for anybody else. No one is selfish enough anymore, goddamnit."

His name was Ghost, or that's what he introduced himself to me as. He was young; his age was tough to distinguish given the scruffy, unkempt beard that came several inches off his chin. We were in a clearing on a piece of private property, sitting on the dirt around a steel fire pit. The sound of a water rushing along the rocks in the river gave a white noise that drowned out any other sounds of the mountains.

Where did that come from? thinking of his statement. "I heard ya, on that one, man." I agreed with him, though I wasn't sure what I was agreeing with.

He begins to tell his story, and I begin to listen to half of it. It turns out Ghost had left everything to come out here. He quit his job and burned all the bridges on the way out. He broke up with his girlfriend, thinking they'd get back together when he was done. "She was supposed to *get it*, ya know? If anyone knew why I had to do this, it was her."

Seems like she didn't get it.

"Guess I gotta do me, before I can do her." It was a stark moment of self-realization until he tacked on "Get it? 'Do her?'" He laughed to himself.

He's got a point though. No one can know what's best for you. Not even your girlfriend whom you thought would 'get it.' Being incoherently selfish has its perks. It's much more fun this way.

I'm back in reality. Ya know, the one where I've been walking for two and a half months, and I am a few thousand miles from home. The reality where I haven't seen another human since I woke up this morning and parted ways with Ghost. The reality where my stomach stopped growling hours ago and is now roaring at me.

I round a bend. And another. And I climb one small peak, descend, and repeat. The air smells so clean.

I regain consciousness from my hiking daze to see a man sitting with his legs out stretched and crossed at the ankles on a small, foldable chair. *That's an odd piece of gear for a thru-hiker.* His bright orange backpack leans against a tree. His jacket matches the color of the pack. He's got a deliberately curled mustache; the rest of his face is just a few days from a clean shave (this isn't exactly the hiker norm). The 'stache is complemented by his dark equally curly, jet black hair that comes down to about his collar. Big aviator sunglasses shine in the late afternoon's light.

"Howdy!" I say. I realize it is the first vocalization I have made in hours.

'Howdy?' What, are you some sort of fucking cowboy? Dude, you're from L.A.

"Good afternoon, friend." He's a warm and welcoming guy.

It is at this point in an addict's life where pleasantries and politeness are thrown out the window. *I just want a nicotine fix.*

I try my best not to sound too desperate. "Hey man, do you happen to have a lighter? Maybe some matches?" *I haven't even asked for this guy's name yet.*

"Totally, man." He reaches into his pocket and pulls out an orange lighter (notice a theme here?) My lack of formality didn't faze him.

I began to take my pack off to find my smokes again, which I deliberately placed on top, just in case I ran into someone. "Winston tastes good, like a cigarette should." He knew an old branding logo for the brand, which I thought was great, so I offered him one, of course. I couldn't tell you if he was a habitual smoker or not, but he took one. Maybe he felt obligated to accept; maybe he was out of smokes himself.

Have you ever had this happen? Where you've just met someone and you've got nothing to talk about after the basic introductions? You know absolutely nothing about the person, and deep down, you don't care to know. You'll never see them again. So, you decide to reflect on your five-minute relationship.

"Damn, I'm lucky to have run into you out in the middle of nowhere."

"Isn't it a crazy coincidence we both smoke?"

"I'm so glad you've got a lighter."

"I'm so glad you've got smokes!"

After our break, we sit in silence for a minute next to each other. I feel so relaxed after every smoke. *This is what it's all about.* I lose myself, looking off into the woods for a long while, taking in my life so far, thinking about how the last few month's decisions led me to having a cigarette break in the forest with a complete stranger. "How far to Pearisburg?" I ask.

"You're trying to get to Pearisburg *tonight*? Dude, you're crazy. You've still got a good," he looked off into the sky as if the answer was just behind his smoke, "seven or eight miles, my friend." My heart sank. My stomach screamed.

With only a few hours of sunlight left, I thanked my savior and was off. Though I did make use of his lighter one last time on the way out. And to be honest, I still don't recall the guy's name.

And now I'm running, almost flying down the trail. I'm famished. *Chinese food. Chinese food. Chinese food.* The final few miles of the trail was a winding series of switchbacks that descended a couple thousand feet in elevation to the small town below.

I can see the town below, but this was the worst kind of false hope. The sun was setting, so I hiked very hurriedly. With air quality so clear and what seemed like a million switchbacks, I could see the town even though I still had a handful of miles to knock out. Time seemed to drag along with my feet.

Now, to this day, I couldn't tell you if this woman ever actually existed but whether or not she did is beside the point. She was my guardian angel.

One more break before I have to get up and go. The sun had completely set. By my best guess, I still had a couple miles to the buffet. I'm now on the interstate that turned into the main street of the small town. I was sitting along the side of the interstate and saw only a car every few minutes.

But the reward I had been pushing for all day no longer was a motivating factor. I couldn't think straight. My head was pounding. I was nauseous to the point where I was sure I was going to throw up. What would have come up though was a mystery. Doubt and homesickness assailed my con-sciousness.

This is mile 500. How will I make it 2200?

How stupid must I have been to end up here without food?

I should have kept hiking with my friends.

I miss my dog.

I miss my sisters.

*I miss my girlfriend. Let's be honest, I just miss the sex. Wait...
let's be more honest, I just miss looking at women. Goddamn.* I
chuckled.

I miss my job? Holy shit, I really do miss that hell hole.

I realize I'm on the verge of crying as soon as an old, beat up
pickup truck pulled over. It braked so quickly the tires squealed in
frustration. It was an early 90's GMC and sounded and looked like it
had been a work truck.

"Hey hiker, you need a lift?"

There might just be a god.

"Thank you!" I toss my backpack into the back of the truck and
hopped into the cab. Now, let's remember that I haven't had a hot
shower in at least a week. I had been hiking every day in the humid
Southern summer. Hikers pack light, so one shirt is all you need.
And deodorant? You can forget about it. Even still, the car reeked of
(you guessed it) cigarette smoke. There was an open beer can in the
cup holder and half a dozen more at my feet.

She was in her mid-fifties. Her hair might have been blonde
once, and her skin might not have looked as much like a football
once too. She was leathery and gross, but my savior nonetheless.

She asks where I'm headed. I ask for her lighter. Other than that,
we were silent the entire time. I was thinking of how badly I must
stink.

Both the beauty and frustration of walking everywhere is how
long it takes to travel 2.5 miles. What would have taken me a little
more than an hour sped by at light speed. She drops me off at the
only hotel in town, never asking my name, where I was from, or
even to have a good night. But she saved me from what would have
been a miserable hour.

I shower very quickly out of politeness to anyone that may end
up eating within a ten-foot radius of me at the rundown lodge and

began the jog down Main Street to the small shopping center with a grocery store, a laundromat, and in all red, capital letters was my Eden.

CHINESE BUFFET.

At least one of the letters was burnt out, if I can recall. The "C" was blinking. It should have been a sign of things to come.

But right now, I'm lighter than air. Everything I want, everything I need is going to be in there: Mountains of fried rice and orange chicken and sweet and sour pork and steamed vegetables!

As I placed my hand on the door to pull open my dreams, I read a sign in the door.

MING'S IS CLOSED ON SUNDAYS.
SORRY FOR INCONVENIENCE.
~Management~

And this is the moment I realize it is Sunday.

About the Author

Alexander D. Francisco is an anthropology student currently attending Fullerton College. This short narrative is based on actual events that happened to Alexander while he hiked the Appalachian Trail in 2013. Since returning from his hiking experience, Alexander has focused on local environmental projects in the community by founding a nonprofit organization to build vegetable gardens throughout Southern California. This is his first published work on print, though other pieces of his work can be found for free on online blogs. He hopes to continue writing and publishing his works while focusing on conservation and environ-mentalism.

The Phone Call

Walter Giles

Life can change in an instant from the time it takes you to blink or even say hello. That's what happened when two young brothers named Buddy and David received a phone call. Unfortunately, that phone call changed their lives forever.

It was a beautiful June morning in bright, sunny Lake Arrowhead. Buddy was getting ready to go to work at a job he had just gotten a few weeks prior. He was struggling to find the perfect outfit to go to work. Trying on shirt after shirt not liking any of the choices he had, nothing looked good on him for the big day. He did that for about half an hour until he finally found the perfect shirt. He was then on his way to his new job. It was something he had been looking forward to all summer. As he jumped into his car, he turned on the radio. Suddenly, his favorite song started to play, so he bumped his music while he made his way along the mountain roads.

When he arrived to his destination, which was The Village, he parked his car and walked to Leroy's Board Shop. He walked in with confidence and greeted all the customers and his fellow co-workers. Straight to the time clock he went and punched his time card. Earlier that morning he had drank a cup of coffee, which led him to his first bathroom break. After finishing his business, he then proceeded to walk around the store and fix items of clothing that had been tampered with. He did that for a couple of hours until his lunch break came around.

For lunch, he walked over to his usual place to eat, Woody's Boathouse, and ordered his favorite club sandwich, with a side of onion rings. He ordered to go and paid his bill; then, he chatted with some friends he had met up with on the way back to Leroy's. Buddy checked his phone to see what time it was before he clocked back in and noticed a missed phone call from his mom. Not thinking anything of it, he proceeded to go back to work. Then, the vibration of his phone shook his pocket, so he checked to see who was calling and the caller I.D. said, 'Mom' so he answered, "Hello?" That's when he got the news…

Beep, Beep, Beep... The alarm from David's phone woke him from his deep slumber. He had only gotten a few hours of sleep because he was up all night celebrating a friend's twenty-first birthday the night before. He checked to see the time and jumped up realizing he had over slept! He had set ten alarms, and it was the last one that finally woke him up. "I'm going to be late to work," he murmured to himself. He quickly jumped into the shower, which made him slip, fall, and stub his toe on the drain. After that, he thought to himself, *How can this day get any worse?* He quickly got out the shower and changed into his Stater Brother's uniform and began to head to work.

Going as fast as he possibly could to make it on time to avoid getting in trouble, he didn't realize there was a highway patrol car parked in a turn out. It was too late, and the blue and red lights were flashing in his rear view mirror. He pulled over and waited for the officer to come to the window to write him a speeding ticket. Afterward, he continued on his way. Being even later to work than he anticipated, he parked his car and ran into the store.

The main manager saw David and yelled, "David, get over here!" David walked over anxiously and his manager asked, "Why are you so late?" He told his manager the entire story starting with the twenty-first birthday party he attended for a friend and ending with the speeding ticket he got just minutes beforehand. The Stater Brother's manager took pity on him and told him to never let it happen again. David then went upstairs to clock in, realizing he was almost an hour late. He then proceeded downstairs to fulfill his duties and also asked one of the cashiers if he needed any assistance with bagging the groceries. The cashier didn't need any assistance, so he went outside and gathered all of the carts that had been left around the lot. He needed the fresh air because he felt sick from the previous night of partying.

After all the carts were rounded up, he went inside and began to check the aisles to see if any of the shelves were cluttered and needed straightening up. Of course, most of the shelves were messed up down every aisle. He continued down all twelve of them making them look nice. After he finished that task, he went to the bathroom during his break. He went to his favorite stall and sat down while he stared at his phone. He was scrolling through Instagram when his phone began to ring and the caller I.D. read, 'Mom,' so he answered. That's when he got the news...

To shed some light on the boys' past, their parents had gotten a divorce while they were the ages of five and three. That led their parents to live in separate households, only a couple minutes' drive from one another. Buddy and David's mom, Yvonne, had recently let a family that was down on their luck move into her home for as long as they needed. The mother of that family name was Beth; she had gone down to Yvonne's room to see if she wanted breakfast, but Yvonne was still sleeping. So, Beth walked back upstairs.

It was then noon, so she went back down to check on Yvonne. She was still asleep, which was a bit odd because she never slept past ten o'clock. Beth continued to check on Yvonne and noticed something wasn't right. She called 911 and requested an ambulance right away. The two young brothers' mother had passed away. As Beth tried to compose herself, she reached for Yvonne's home phone and called Buddy and David.

About the Author

Walter Giles was born and raised in Running Springs, California, a small town in the San Bernardino Mountains. His family is his biggest inspiration, including his five-month-old son. He would like to have an aspiring career in business while also enjoying his hobbies, such as skateboarding, snowboarding, and down time with his family. He wrote this story to remind all people that no matter how good or how bad your day one phone call could change your life in an instant. This story is dedicated to his mother Yvonne Marie Giles.

My Life of Change and Victory

Maria Guzman

Professionally working for many years in a private for profit company and then within the non-profit agency business has given me the opportunity to professionally grow and learn, but it has also made me a kinder human being. One of my most recent work experiences has really impacted my life: an opportunity to work for a work source center with a behind the scenes shelter for women who were victims of domestic violence. I was given the opportunity by someone I will call an angel, who on a daily basis saw me going into the work source center applying and searching for employment for about a month, before being offer a job opportunity. I would go in after dropping of my son in school and not leaving the work source center until it was time to pick up my child from school. The career advisor on site offered the job opportunity as a transitional housing case manager position. Working for non-profit agency, I was able to work in various positions including transitional shelter case manager, emergency shelter case manager, and as a counselor/advocate.

Working as a social services case manager, I was able to learn of the many challenges abused women endure, not only with life struggles, but also the abuse endured by either their domestic partners, violent family members, and even sometimes their own fathers. The worst part of the abuse is when children are exposed to these abusive relationships. After being sent to various trainings including D.C.F.S. Department of Children Services, 40-hour domestic violence, court process, D.V. counselor advocate and other many trainings. I felt ready and happy to be able to assist someone in need of guidance and hope. But, I also realized domestic violence is a very strong subject that society does not like to deal with.

However, domestic violence is a terrible crime that no one should go through. Domestic violence is a vicious cycle that only continues to escalate if the cycle is not broken. Domestic violence does not know any barriers. Women and men with education or no education endure abuse, whether it is physical, emotional, mental, economical and sexual. Abuse can also exist in same sex relationship. Throughout my case management experience with such cases, I had to type case scenarios including details that were so dramatic and traumatizing. In one particular scene, an abusive partner was giving drugs to his wife, who often felt tired and slept most of the time, so that the abuser could sexually abuse the children. In another case, a young woman who was not even eighteen yet was forced to run away with her abusive boyfriend, only to end up homeless and pregnant while her abusive partner forced her to have sex in public places. In another situation, I received a hot-line call from a young man who was being physically abused by his older male partner. Several calls were made to assist the young man who had mentioned wanting to commit suicide. There is not enough shelter for LGBT, lesbians, gay, bi-sexual, transgender.

The most ironic of this life experience is that my own family had suffered such events. My own mother had been physically, emotionally and mentally abused by her own father. A particular abusive episode I recalled is when I saw my mother sitting in a chair crying quietly, while my father was arguing, slapping her and burning her arms with his cigarette, while he was smoking. This continue for what seemed to me hours.

During that incident, my little sister and I were hiding in our room. Spying through the bedroom door was something I often did. On another occasion, my father and mother had been arguing over something I can't recall what the issue was, but it was intense because I saw my father running after my mother. My father seemed to be sadistic, because on that particular day my mother had finished taking a shower and was about put her clothes on. Therefore, my mother was running away from my father, with only a towel wrapped around her body. He did manage to pull her towel, while she was trying to get away from going back into the house. My father was often taking me and younger sister to other girlfriends' houses, while my mother worked to earn a living. My father was never aggressive with me or my sister, yet he was a total different man.

I was born in Mexico and raised by grandparents until I was four years old. During that time, both of my parents were in South Gate, CA. My parents were very young and lacked the maturity to make wise decisions needed to create a loving family. Yet, my mother and father had decided to relocate to the United States without any idea of what life would turn out to be. Once each was established with a job and able to get an apartment, they also seemed to get along and make new friends and other not-too-good acquaintances, which later would cause great damage in my parents' lives and relationship. After getting established, quickly my mother sent for me and my life was changed- abruptly. I quickly realized I had a little sister and anew set of parents I hardly knew.

Living in the United States was not easy. I missed both my grandparents and my cousins so much, and according to my mother, I was taken to the doctor because I did not want to eat. I was full of sadness; I almost died according to what my mother mentioned. However, my mother was very resourceful and planned a way to make me eat. After a few months, learning to live a different life with my parents was inevitable. However, after several years, my parents were divorced and my mother continued working to provide for her family. Today, she is hairdresser and likes the DIY project. And as for me, I am going to school to further my education and majoring in psychology. I have two wonderful sisters and two great brothers. I live with my husband and my adorable ten-year-old daughter and sweetheart son who is twenty-four years of age.

About the Author

Maria Guzman is presently a student at College of the Desert.

Mountain of the Dead

Mariah Halbert

"This story is dedicated to my God, my loved ones, and to the nine skiers that died that night during the Daytlov Pass Incident."

~Mariah Halbert

*Some of these events are based on a true story.

On a cold, snowy January morning, ten skilled hikers embark on a journey. Most of them were grad students, and Igor Dyatlov plans for this hiking trip to be a difficult one, but only to train these students into doing much more difficult trips. These two girls and eight men begin to pack up their things, such as cameras, notebooks, sleeping bags, and clothing, as well as skis for the journey ahead. Little did they know what would be in store for them. They say their goodbyes and give love to their loved ones. They pack everything in the trucks and head for the train station.

A day passes, and they arrive at the station. It is after sunset, so they stay the night in a hotel nearby and sleep. With banging and shouting, Dyatlov bangs on the frying pan and yells, "Wake up! It's time to move!" With the moans and groans, each of the students climbs out of bed to get ready to board the train. Yuri Yudin wakes up with a thumping in his head and an urge to throw up. Even though he feels very weak, he tries to hop out of bed and run to the bathroom! As hard as he tries to hold it in, he throws up on Zinaida.

"Oh no, I'm so sorry, Zinaida!" Yuri says.

"Oh, it's alright. Accidents happen," Zinaida tries to say reassuringly. "Maybe you should not go with us. You don't look well, and we all wouldn't want you to be miserable."

With the stench of vomit in the room, they all pack up while Yuri tries to clean up his mess. Once all of that is done, they say goodbye to Yuri and drive to the train station.

Once they arrive, the students and Igor grab their backpacks and board the train. With the sound of the horn and the grinding of the wheels, they are off! The girls share one room, and the boys split into two other rooms. Once the girls have their beds made up, they sit for a while looking out into the beautiful scenery passing them. The sky is dark and gloomy, and big white snowflakes are falling effortlessly. The room is filled with a sweet smell of polished wood and cinnamon, and the room is lit with a flickering light from the candle and lantern.

"So, what are you most excited about for this trip?" asks Zinaida.

"I'm very excited to do what I love with all of you guys, but especially going through the Otorten Mountain range! I've seen pictures, and I've heard it is beautiful! But also I've heard it has an eerie atmosphere, and I don't mind that stuff," responds Lyudmila.

Zinaida says, "You don't mind that kind of feeling? I don't like any creepy or scary things, but I feel safe enough with the guys. I do feel bad for Yuri. I know how badly he wanted to go. I know he has been planning for this trip for a while."

"Well that's why we brought cameras and journals! We will take many photos and write down what we see and our progress every day, so then when he reads and sees the pictures, he can somewhat get the experience." Lyudmila says.

"That is true. I think he will appreciate it greatly." Zinaida says. With that, they get into their beds and try to get as much sleep as they can.

The girls wake up, and outside the sky is still dark and gloomy. They get up and go into one of the boy's rooms. In there Rustem, Georgyi, and Nicolas are awake.

"How did you boys sleep?" asks Zinaida.

"Good, but it was pretty chilly for me," responds Nicolas. "But how did you ladies sleep?"

"Very well. I felt pretty comfortable," says Lyudmila. As Zinaida is about to speak, Igor enters the room.

"I hope all of you slept well. Have your stuff ready in fifteen minutes. Once you're done, meet me in my room," and then he exits.

So the girls go back into their room and pack up their things as well as the other boys. As they finish, they turn of the lanterns and blow out the candles and go to Dyatlov's room. Within a couple of minutes of going into the room, the conductor speaks into the speakers, "We are now approaching Otorten Mountain range. For those of you leaving us, be ready to exit at your nearby exits. Thank you." The train stops, the conductor sounds the horn, and the doors open. All of them hop out and put their backpacks on and gather around just before the tree line.

"Alright, everyone. Let's get this hike started! If we stay at a good speed and try to not take very many stops, we can get to Vizhai within three days." Igor says.

"But first, let's take a group picture!" yells Lyudmila. Everyone huddles up and gets into position while Lyudmila runs to get a good distance to take the picture. It's overcast, and the snow on the ground looks like it is glowing. Big snowflakes continue to fall silently and the trees create a beautiful backdrop with its rich green pine needles and dark brown trunks. "Ready? One, two THREE! Thanks guys!" yells Lyudmila. Once she runs back over, they line up and start their hike.

A day into their hike, with a day and a half left to reach Vizhai, they make great progress. As they continue to hike, Rustem stops causing Alexander and Nicolas to stop as well.

"Hey, wait. Don't you guys feel like something is following us?" says Rustem. No one responds for a moment, but Nicolas responds, "Kind of. Who knows, it might be a bear. We will just have to keep an eye out and just be more cautious."

Then out in the woods to the left of them, there is a large roar! Lyudmila and Zinaida scream and grab each other, and the men all scream too and look frantically in the direction it came from. These are all experienced hikers, and they know their animal sounds. But for a fact, they knew this was from something else, much bigger than a bear, but also sounded like a man. They all huddle together back to back looking for the thing that made the roar. But nothing else came from the woods. It was silent, and there was an eerie feeling in the air. They try to decide if they should go back down the range, or continue to Vizhai, and they decide they had made so much progress, and it would be longer to go back down then to continue to Vizhai, so they continue onward.

The hikers move on with extra caution, looking around every moment to see if that thing was in the open, but there was nothing. Night quickly falls, and they decide to make camp. As they set up their tents, out in the distance there is a big crackle and a thud. It sounded as if a large tree had fallen down, and then they hear the same roar as they did earlier in the day.

Everyone screams again, and Igor yells out, "Quickly!! Grab your bags and run out into the open!" Everyone screams, and they frantically try to pack their things and start to run. Zinaida takes out her camera and tries to take pictures. She randomly takes a shot in that direction and another one in that direction, but little did she know that she took one of the creature. All of them keep running, and they break out of the shelter of the woods and are now in the open. They stop and look back into the woods and wait for movement or even a sound. It is quite yet again, and they decide to put more distance between them and the woods.

So a mile away from the tree line, they set up the tent the girls had been sharing since they left the other one where they ran from and all sit together. Lyudmila takes out her journal, puts the date at the top, and frantically writes down all she could think of. From when they first heard the noise to when they started to set up camp then made a mad dash out of the woods to get into the open.

Then, she remembers olds stories of what her grandfather said and other elderly men and women. The Yeti, or also called the snowman, is half man and half gorilla, and it is very tall. It can grow up to the height of eight feet and is very hairy. It has the roar of a bear, but it has some qualities of a human. While she thinks about this, Georgyi interrupts her thoughts and whispers, "Can you hear that?"

He takes out his pocket knife, and cuts a hole in the canvas of the tent big enough for him to look out of and stares out into the darkness. Then he whispers, "I see something." Lyudmila pushes him out of the way to look, and she sees it! It is big with massive shoulders and is very tall. It is hairy, and she realizes it's the Yeti.

She moves over and writes down in her journal, '...*and now we know the snowman exists.*'

As Igor yells the Yeti yells and starts running toward the tent. Everyone starts to scream and tries to find their way out of the tent. The men cut more holes, and they rip it open, and everyone starts to run. The black of the night causes them to not see very well, and they run past the Yeti and back into the woods. They all meet up and try to make a fire, so they can see. Both Lyudmila and Zinaida are crying, and the boys are trying to catch their breath and try to think of a plan. They don't have big weapons; all they have are knives.

Rustem makes a fire illuminating about eight feet around them. In only a matter of seconds, they can hear the Yeti running toward the light. Out of nowhere, there is a crackle and tree falling only a foot away from them. And that same roar comes from where that crackle is. The students scatter. Three of them run toward the open, three more go along the edge of the tree line, and the other three try to desperately climb massive pine trees. But one by one the students are picked off. The great strength that came from the Yeti was too much for them to handle. The cries of pain and pure fear are cut off one by one as the Yeti kills them.

As days pass by with no word from any of the hikers, loved ones demand for a search and rescue. As helicopters are sent out over the Mountain of the Dead, one of the pilots sees something odd down below. They pick out a landing spot, and as they get closer, they see the tent the students had been in. They radio in they found something, and all of the rescue team eventually makes it to the spot. The sun is bright, and there is snow all around. As they see in the tent, all of the belongings to the students were still there, but no one was in there. They search miles around and soon enough one by one they find the bodies of the students. They did not know what caused this, but as the investigation goes on, they could not find what caused this since the evidence made no sense. The deaths of the students cause experts to be dumb-founded, and the deaths remain inconclusive.

About the Author

Mariah Halbert lives in Southern California and is in her first semester of college. She loves to be involved in her church youth group and enjoys being with children. She loves playing volleyball and being outdoors. Mariah loves her family, boyfriend, and friends. But above all, God comes first in her everyday life.

This Dear Skin of Mine

Fernando Lescano

"We must live together as brothers or perish as fools."
- Martin Luther king Jr.

What defines a person? Is it morals? Is it wealth? Or is it the size of the heart? Several times, I have asked myself these questions as I reminisced of my childhood. As long as I could remember, I would get called different names as well as be judged by the color of my skin. As time went on, it would become a part of me that I would become ashamed of. Soon thereafter, I would wish I were born with white skin. Unfortunately, wishful thinking doesn't get you very far in life. You have to play the cards you are dealt with in life and plan your next move of attack. I instead went into defense mode, by finding new ways to become a new person. Time as well as life would truly show me what it meant to bare this dear skin of mine.

One cloudy Monday afternoon, some sixteen years ago, I was waiting in line after recess with my classmates, for our teacher to take count and guide us back to class. I remember standing there hoping we would get to go to the library that day. I had been waiting anxiously for the new *Harry Potter* book by J.K Rowling. I would check the school library windows every morning after breakfast every day, hoping the announcement poster would be displayed. Well, after countless days of checking every morning, hoping to see the display change from coming soon to now available, it had finally arrived. There it was clear as day, the Harry Potter poster with the words 'now available' in big letters.

There was very little I wanted to remember from that day, but I distinctly remember wearing my favorite blue sweater with green paw prints. I loved that sweater, and I wore it almost every day, along with dark denim jeans and a pair of sneakers with mini Pikachu's on them. Standing right behind me was Stephanie Wishek and Samantha O'Conner giggling to each like always. I could not help but overhear Stephanie say in a whisper, "My mommy said that they are brown like that because they do not shower. I bet you if Fernando would shower, the water would turn black." It was then followed by an obnoxious giggle. Samantha giggled and said, "No wonder he always smells." Their giggles were getting louder than a whisper at that point. Samantha then took a step back and said,

"Don't get too close to him. He might make you throw up from the smell." I stood there not saying a single word and kept my face forward with no expression. But deep down inside, my heart was sinking. My face felt hot and my eyes swelled up, and I could not help but let a tear fall from my face.

Later that night, I scrubbed my skin over and over again, hoping it would turn white. Instead, it broke open, and the water ran bright red. I stood there in the shower not knowing the difference between my tears and the warm water hitting my sore skin. I stood there wondering, *Why me? Why this skin? Why am I being judged and treated like a freak? Over something I can never change.* Later, I would find that that would not be the only thing I would not be able to change. My heart was filled with pain and sentiment for what had happened at school. I still could not believe what those girls had said in line after recess. Their words would haunt my thoughts thereafter and would hurt me in more ways than I would ever imagine.

My mother later found me, in my room draped with a blood-stained towel. She immediately thought the worst, as she ran to me and asked me over and over again, "Who did this to you?" Each time I stayed quiet, until I heard her cry and say, "Why would anybody hurt my handsome son like this? Please tell me who do this to you, honey please!" It was then that I broke and cried out with anger, "I did because my skin is dirty and gross! But no matter how hard I scrub, I cannot get my skin clean and white." I then turned and looked at mother and saw a look I would never forget. It was one of concern, disbelief, and hurt. It brought tears to my eyes to see her in such pain. She looked straight at me and asked in an almost broken voice, "Who told you that lie?" I looked away in shame and said, "Some girls at school," with tears falling from my face. My mother then said, "God made you in His image and loves you this way, and that's all that matters." She then kissed my forehead, dressed my scratches, helped me into my pajamas, and tucked me into bed.

The next morning, I woke up and felt silly for what I had done. Regret set in as well. When I began to get ready for school, my skin was so sore and oily from the antibiotic cream my mom had put on my skin the night before. As my mother walked me to the bus stop, she said, "So not listen to what those girls have to say. You just stay focused in school." I just looked at my mother, nodded, and replied, "Yes, Mother." But in my head, I could not help but feel hopeless and think if only it were that simple. I pulled my hoodie over my head and kept to myself. I sat there praying and hoping that the day would go by fast and that nobody else would ever notice me again, which was kind of hard when I stuck out like a sore thumb in a primarily white school.

My childhood sweater would one day turn black and become my safe haven from the world. I would wear it like my skin, and it would follow me wherever I would go like my shadow. It would help me get through the day knowing my skin was out of sight and out of mind. *My poor dear skin*, I thought as I grew older. *Why must I be afraid to show my true colors? Why must the world be so cruel? Why must I live in fear of people's deepest darkest intentions?* I wondered at age twelve when I grew tired of my black sweater. I continued to grow restless. The true me wanted to grow by getting rid of my sweater, become someone new, and live a new and exciting life, a life where the only thing to fear was fear itself. I thought of all of these things while I sat there at the lunch the table like always.

To this day, I still cannot believe what happened next. Out of nowhere, a friendly face sat right next to me and said, "Hey, I'm new here in school. I moved here from Arizona. Do you mind if I sit here with you?" I simply nodded yes. He then turned and said, "Nice sweater, but aren't you hot? It's like ninety degrees out here. I'm sweating here just looking at you. Why don't you take it off, dude?" I froze. I could not believe what I was hearing. It was almost as if God had sent a sign. I didn't give it another thought. I took my sweater of freeing me from my insecurities and opening up a whole new world.

About the Author

Fernando Lescano is a Health science major. He was born and raised in Redlands and have lived there practically all his life. He frequently visited Mexico where he spent all his summers and sometimes his winter breaks with his grandmother. When his grandmother and aunt became ill during his sophomore year, he left Redlands to care for them both. A year later, his aunt died and soon after his grandmother. That made him want to pursue nursing, and he opened his heart to be there for this sick and injured. His plans are to transfer with an Associate's in Health Science to a four year university and continue on to become a Nurse Practitioner. He is currently working in a retirement community in their health center as a certified nurse assistant. He is a licensed cosmetologist and works at a salon as a hair stylist. Art and care have always been his passion and he hopes to one do great things in this world.

Fairuz, Oranges, Resistance

Moné Makkawi

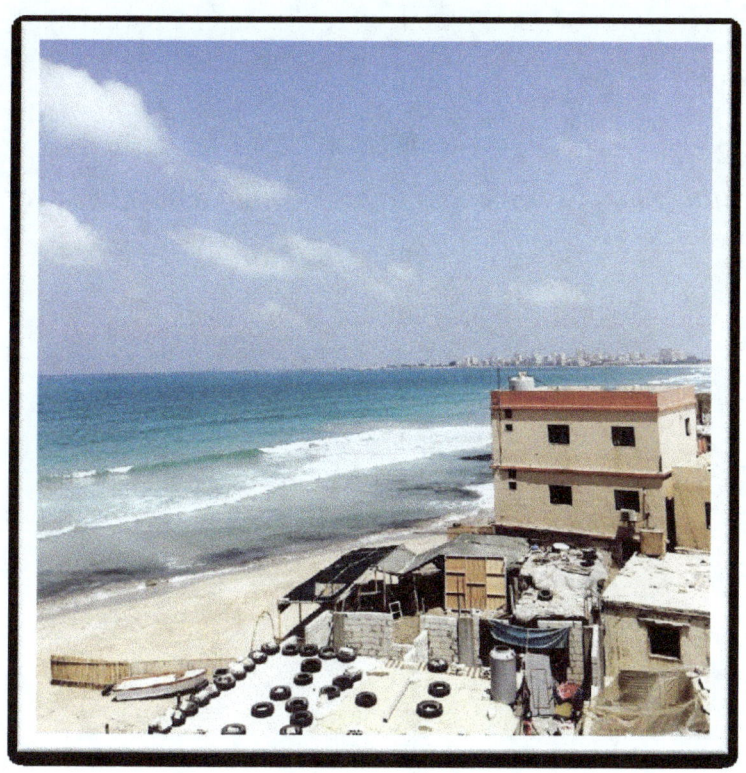

"Be a reverse terrorist.

Plot. Plan. Scheme and launch random acts of Love.

Incite it. Invite it. Ignite it.

Shake this world to its foundation.

And enjoy yourself in the process."

Robert Mann

Hello, everyone. This is your pilot speaking. We are beginning our descent into Beirut; local time is 4:45 PM....

The rest is fuzz and static because all I can focus on is that I'm home! Eventually we land, and everyone eagerly exits the plan. The next half an hour is a fuzzy muddle of customs, passport stamps, baggage claim, and getting myself together. Then, I walk out of the very small terminal.

It's just like I remembered; I walk out of the one and only exit of Beirut's tiny airport. I turn a corner, and I'm greeted by a crowd of families, friends, extended relatives waiting to see the familiar faces of their loved ones. I'm not the one they're looking for, so I keep walking. Eventually, I see the driver I'm supposed to meet up with. He's holding a sign with my name on it. I'm feeling famous, and I greet him in Arabic.

"How are you? Moné right?"

"Good! Yes, that's me!" I laughed a combination of nervousness and excitement.

"I'm Abu Ali. Good to meet you. This is Jay. He'll be going to the south with us."

"Nice to meet you both. I'm ready to go whenever you both are!"

I shake jovial Abu Ali's hand and hug Jay. We talked the past couple days on Facebook. It feels natural, and we're friends already. We walk to our car, and as I'm walking, it all comes rushing back: the smells, the sights, the sounds. It's hot and humid. I hear a symphony of honking cars. I'm surrounded by an eclectic mix of Mercedes Benzes from circa 1970 in assorted mint greens, mustard yellows, periwinkle blues and the rare black.

Home.

As we drive, I kick back with the cigarette Jay handed me, because you know, when in Rome. I admire Beirut's outline. The windows are all open, so the warm Mediterranean wind is blowing my hair all crazy around my face. It smells like the beach all around me, and the sun is setting, so it's not hot at all at this point.

To my left are hills and mountains, dotted as far up as you can see with apartment complexes, no traditional houses, and bullet-ridden buildings. With half-bombed habitats, the city has taken on war, violence, and heartache to make its own architecture. To my right is the beautiful Mediterranean. Right now, it's awash in a pink-orange glow because the sun is setting, and the wispy clouds are floating in the same soft palette of colors. The water is light blue and twinkling, winking at me because it knows I've come back to it, and we are sharing this moment.

We talk to pass the time of the hour and a half drive. Jay is cool. He's from Canada, originally New Jersey I find out, and he tells me about what he's studying in school. Abu Ali too is a friendly character, and we all joke about the traffic and army checkpoints we repeatedly drive through because it's normal. Before I know it we are in Tyre, the southern-most major city in Lebanon. It's dark, and I get dropped off at our apartment. I randomly realize I'm lucky it's dark because I wore shorts for the flight and forgot to change into a more modest outfit.

At this point, I'm getting settled and introducing myself to the girls and guys who are already there. Boys and girls apartments are separated to respect the cultural norms of the small, predominantly Shi'a community we are staying in. I meet the girls with whom I'm sharing a room, and they are nice, kind, the whole nine yards. I'm excited to go to bed, not because I'm tired but because I want a new day to begin! We have orientation tomorrow, and the day following, we begin teaching.

A new day. Today, we all had breakfast together in the center of the camp where some of us will be teaching, and then we jumped right into preparing. About thirty of us volunteers are stuffed in a small theater room. It's hot, humid, and close quarters, but we press on. We talk about why we're here: we are teaching English in the Palestinian refugee camps of Lebanon for two reasons: first off, to give these children tools for empowerment. I didn't realize it before this, but in this land, the country I hold so dear to my heart for so many different reasons, these refugees who were forced out of their homeland in 1948 have no rights in my own homeland. I didn't know it, but they can't even go to school, can't work in most professions, and can't even own land. They're all confined to these camps.

What the literal fuck? How did I not know about all this shit?

So, we're talking about education. It's important. Yeah, I obviously know this. But, we talk more and more about it, and I'm still learning. We talk about ways to teach the kids and work with them, and we move on to other topics, but the ideas are still lingering with me.

If I'm going to be analytical, I can reflect and understand I'm learning a lot of things today, and even though I knew why I was coming (namely to teach), I'm getting a newfound idea of the impact my role here will have and how seriously I need to take these next few weeks. We've done a lot of discussion today about our roles, and I'm starting to realize the immense impact I could possibly have as a teacher here, serving this community.

Looking around at the mix of new people around me, I feel humble and lucky to have been brought in to this small, private community. I feel like I'm seeing a side of the world most people won't ever see, and from that understanding, I'm feeling the weight of a service owed to these people who let me in. I'm making a vow to myself right now for these next few weeks, I am here for the children. It's all about the children, and my job is to provide them with the tools to empower themselves.

The next thing on our orientation agenda is to hear stories from refugees who fled Palestine in 1948. We go downstairs as a group. I don't know what to expect; I've learned about the exodus of Palestinians, the fleeing, terror, and all that, but I've never met someone who has lived through these events and witnessed them.

I'm in the camp, and I'm surrounded at this point by daughters, sons, grandchildren of an expelled people, but I don't really feel the magnitude. We're seated in front of an elderly man dressed in the traditional clothing of a *hajj* and *hajja* (one who has completed the pilgrimage to Mecca), and I'm eager to hear what they have to say.

The refugees both tell heartbreaking stories, stories of their lives before their lives were scattered, their farms, villages, crops and lives... experiencing the *Nakba* (disaster), pre-imposed Diaspora.

I'm feeling torn, sad, nostalgic even. I listen to their stories, and I'm transported. I listen to the anguish in the *hajj's* voice as he talks about the fact that his history and lineage and his future all continue to be defined by life in the camps now.

At this point, I'm feeling a building sense of sadness. I thought I was there, that I realized the gravity of my place and what I needed to do... but then Mahmoud spoke. He started off almost timid, an uncertain addition out of respect for his elders, not thinking he had something of weight to say. But his interjection has a lasting effect on me and visibly, on everyone throughout the tiny, still room. In slow Arabic, he says:

> "My grandfather was refugee from the Nakba. My father lived in these same camps, and I live here too. My children probably will as well. Generation after generation experience this, and it's not going away. There are people going to the moon, achieving great things, and we're here worrying about having running water or working electricity."

Wow, that hit. Those sentences, that sentiment. It stuck with me the rest of summer, and I felt it would the rest of my life. I'm feeling with these people now, not only sympathizing, but also empathizing. On such a basic level, these are my brothers and sisters. These humans are suffering, and until now I've done nothing at all. I honestly feel like I'm barely doing anything now. All I'm doing is thinking, and I feel lost in all these thoughts. I don't think I've been struck by an idea or feeling like that in so long. I wanted to continue orientation, to continue preparing myself, if not to get a break from such a heavy feeling.

We were back at the apartment, and I'm talking with Jessica, another teacher. I'm talking about what we heard today and hearing the refugees speak. All of a sudden, I see her start to cry.
"What is the point? Seriously what is the point of what we're doing here?"

I'm taken aback, and I pause before answering. "Jess, it will, I mean, slowly but…"

"Nothing is going to change, these poor kids, and nothing is going to change."

I didn't really know what to say to her because honestly, after today, I'm feeling the same way. So, we just sat there together in silence as the electricity cut out for the fifth time that night.

The next few days, we whizzed through orientation. Before I knew it, it was time for the first day of classes. The initial day of class has finally arrived, after a couple days of curriculum training and discussions. To say I'm feeling nervous is a little bit of an understatement. I'm sweating, which could be attributed to the 87-degree weather and 40 percent humidity today, but it could be nerves just the same.

We arrive at the camp for the day and walk to the back of the center to see the kids lined up for us and waiting. The program director of the center, Mahmoud, announces some things in Arabic about the day and tells the kids to prepare to sing. *I wonder what they'll be singing?*

They sing a beautiful anthem for Palestine, steadfastness, freedom and courage. I stand there watching the kids. They're so tiny, but they stand with their chests puffed out and their bodies straight and strong. I don't know any of them yet, but I'm feeling weirdly proud and one hundred percent possessed by the strength of these kids' spirits.

All the teachers begin walking towards their respective rooms with their children at this point. I'm getting anxious because the moment we've been building up the past few weeks has come. My kids and I get to our classroom, and they all sit down; I start handing out their notebooks and paper.

Time slows down... I get to the front of the classroom and turn around to face all the kids I'm going to get to know over the next five weeks... For about thirty seconds, I actually freeze:
Oh fuck, what have I done. I'm all alone with these kids, and I don't know what to do! Where do I start? Where's my lesson plan? Oh, my God! They know I'm nervous. They can smell it. That tiny one is mad-dogging me. I'm so screwed.

They're all staring at me with expectant faces, and finally I speak: "Ok, guys. Open up your workbooks to page two, please." I said something! We've started!

We work throughout the day. We do some basic activities, grammar drills, just to see where the kids are, even though they've taken a diagnostic exam. The kids are so bright! They don't know much English, but besides all the fooling around (Majid threw at least five erasers across the room at Fadi), the kids seem like they actually enjoy what we're doing. I'm teaching, and they are actually learning (I hope).

A week has passed. Classes are going amazingly. They continue to inspire/frustrate me to no end. We're taking the kids to a small river today (a small, polluted, Lebanese watering hole) to get them out of the camps, a reward for working so hard in classes as well. It was so much fun.
We rolled up to the spot, all couple hundred kids and us volunteers. It was a small river surrounded on either side by high hills and a swirling blue sky. Compared to the calm outside, it was chaos within the bus: the kids were yelling, screaming, jumping up and down.

We unloaded the bus, and it was an instant party. We spent all day playing, splashing each other, eating, drinking, playing soccer, taking pictures (a million of them), laughing, singing, and dancing. Someone brought a tabla (drum), and before I could blink, our students had formed a circle to dance dabke (a traditional Palestinian dance).

I don't know where it came from, but I came alive! Normally, I'm not a big dancer, but the spirit of these kids possessed me. I don't know, I felt it, and I wanted to dance all day with them. We whirled around like water and clouds, and we were all kids. I saw the biggest grins on tiny faces today, just a short drive away made the world to all the little ones.

When we left, the green hills on either side of us looked so beautiful. The water was still with no children in it anymore, and the water had a calming color and feel of moss.

Today, the curriculum is emotions. I feel like these might be easy to teach the kids, but I've learned the past couple weeks that whenever I think that, I'm usually wrong. Everyone is filing in: Fadi, Mohammad, Hadi, Zara, Damooa, Ahmed, other Mohammad. All twenty of the little ones sit down, and we begin.

"Good morning, everyone!"

"Good morning, teacher!"

I begin talking about emotions, describing them in Arabic. There are some complicated ones to get to, but for now I start with the basics. "Okay, everyone. Does anyone know what happy means?" Because of the translations in their workbooks, all the kids shout out, "s3id!" in Arabic.

We talk about what makes us happy. Some kids say going to the sea. A lot of boys in the class say playing soccer.

"How about angry or sad?" It's become a game now, and the kids all scream out, "z3lehn!" (Upset). I ask again for examples, but what the kids start to say freezes me. One of my favorites, Omar, speaks up: "It makes me mad that I can't go back to Palestine. It makes me sad that my family is here in the camps." Most of the kids nod along. A girl stands up, Aya, and says, "I'm sad that the world doesn't like us, and we can't play like normal kids." I don't really have much to say to them, but I know I should say something. All I'm thinking of is what Mahmoud said on the first day.

"It's not fair, I know. You guys are here, and other people can travel and do whatever they want. But, you're all learning. You're only kids and you're learning English, and you have dreams right? Who wants to be a doctor when they grow up?"

Six hands go up.

"Who wants to be a teacher?"

Ten hands go up.

"See! You can all become whatever you want! You can't let where you are now decide where you are going."

The kids all start talking amongst themselves. To cement the idea and finish classes for the day, I ask them all to draw what they want to be when they grow up, so we can put the pictures up all around the classroom to see every day.

As all the kids leave, I collect their pictures, a lot of pictures of doctors, teachers, and most of all, pictures of Palestine. They all had words like freedom, love, and we will return. A lot of them had el-3wda drawn on them (the key representing the Palestinian right of return). I felt a little said, but I felt more hopeful.

The kids have nothing really with them in the camps. The sewage runs through the streets. Often, they don't have electricity or running water. Their host country, my sweet Lebanon, doesn't even grant them civil rights. But they are politicized from the moment they can remember. They are fighting for an idea from the moment they can walk. These kids are all braver than anyone I know. They're continuing the spirit of return just by being themselves, by learning and having their ideas and dreams. It got me to thinking that the least I can do is join them in the cause and devote all I can to it.

I start to put up their pictures around a piece of paper I wrote a quote on and hung up the first day of classes. It's an Assata Shakur quote, and it reads, "No one is going to give you the education you need to overthrow them. Nobody is going to teach you your true history, teach you your true heroes, if they know that that knowledge will help set you free."

I'm saying goodbye to the kids and teachers at the center today. We're having a final ceremony where the kids can show off what they learned during the last five weeks. One girl performs a crazy good rap about Palestine she wrote herself (she's ten years old by the way) in creative writing class. Our theater class performs a small play they brainstormed and co-wrote themselves, in English, of course.

Parents, family, and friends are here. It's a beautiful sight to see so many people crammed into a small, hot room just to see the shining moments of these kids. As I watch them all perform and talk, I feel like a mom. I never thought I'd feel like a mom 'til I was actually a mom, but maybe I kind of am a mom now. I watch my kids beaming with pride, performing their very own *Macbeth*'s and displaying their very own *Starry Night's*.

After the ceremony, my kids all come up to me with little presents I know they bought with their own money from the sheer pride on their little faces: a tiny necklace from Rena and a note from Samih that says, "I love you, teacher."

I hug a million hugs, and say, "Goodbye for now (not for good)" to all of them. As the last few are leaving, Omar comes up to me and asks in English, "Teacher, you are coming back next year?" I laugh, high five him, hug him, and say, "Of course!"

About the Author

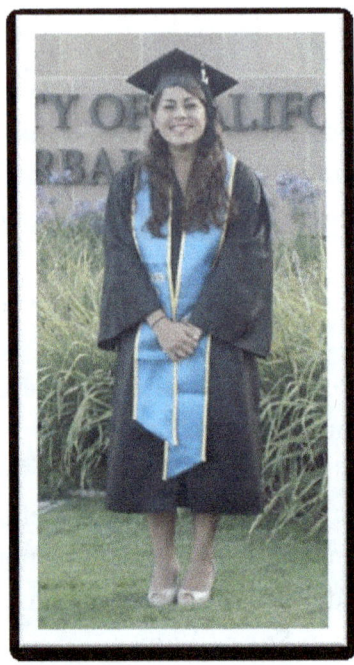

Moné Makkawi is a recent graduate from the University of California, Santa Barbara. She is a lover of life! She is also currently applying to graduate programs in Middle Eastern studies. She hopes to continue writing and spreading awareness about the plight of international refugees, Palestinians, and the situation abroad in the Middle East. Free Palestine and good vibes to all!

Crazy-Haired Susie

Stacey Ogden

Self-Discovery

Heaven on ear; Peace in our minds.

Silence is nice; calmness is bliss.

Trust in yourself, and everything as is.

Cherish the love, and remember to give.

The life we choose to live is the one that will exist.

Every free moment could be a change from within.

Openness is the passage way in.

~Stacey Ogden

Meet little Susie. She had the craziest curly hair. Little crazy-haired Susie lived in a huge castle on top of the hill, away from the rest of the world. She liked where she lived but didn't understand why she was kept away from everyone else. Susie was a strange girl; she always claimed she felt alone in a room full of people, but the only people she knew were the ones that worked in the castle. She never had any friends and grew accustomed to her solitude.

She grew up with loving parents and a wild love for the earth and everything on it. She would play in the back garden climbing trees and playing in the grass. She would be in the garden from sun up to sun down. She would look at the city down below, longing to be a part of whatever was going on down there.

As little Susie grew older, the wonder of the world never left her. She knew she had to venture off into the unknown. She knew leaving the castle was against her parents' wishes. They felt the world would eat her alive. Susie was a beautiful young lady, and her parents wanted her to marry into royalty or wealth. If she left, she would never be able to come back to the comforts she once knew. It would be a journey for a lifetime. She knew in the depths of her soul her destiny would be a great one.

As she left for her journey, she let her family know that she was not coming back. Her decision shamed the family's wishes. She was meant to spend her life in the castle, but Susie knew that was not the life she wanted. She gathered up a few belongings and set off to the world. She took with her enough food for a few days, some clothes, a blanket, and some of her jewelry to trade. As she left, her mother warned her of troubles she would face, and if she ever wanted to come back, she was always welcome.

She began on her journey into town. She decided to walk; it would take her two days. As she arrived into town, she began to get nervous. There were so many people doing many different things all at once. There were people in dirty clothes selling trinkets that were spread on blankets. There was a sad older man with no legs asking for money. There were kids running through the street playing soccer. Susie had never imagined all this could be going on all at once, all the sounds and commotions. She knew at that moment that is where she wanted to be.

Susie found a little hotel where she could trade some of her jewelry for a place to stay. They offered her job, helping to clean rooms and cooking in the kitchen. That is exactly what Susie needed to start her life. She knew she didn't need much just enough to pay for her rooms and food. That was a huge blessing for Susie. It was as if they knew she was going to be coming; the timing couldn't have been more perfect.

As little Susie got older, the more life made sense, and her hair became less crazy. The things she was doing started to make a path for her. She would give to the world time, love, companionship, and an unrelenting amount of patience. She would talk to the moon and stars. She would look optimistically into the morning sun, for morning was her favorite time of day. She proclaimed that the trees would guide her to her path, as they always have, and she would walk barefoot on that path, trusting the ground she walked on and feeding on its energy.

Little Susie had a wanderer's heart, always looking for adventure in life. She had given herself her God, trusting her path. She knew the guidance of her good deeds would take her to the enlightenment she was seeking. She tried to learn everything she possibly could about people and herself. She began making friends and started feeling she was becoming a part of her community. She loved her family she had left behind in the castle, but she knew she had to make a life of her own, and she was succeeding at that.

Even though Susie never understood others, she always loved people. She felt like she had something to give to the world. What the crazy-haired girl had to give was kindness and love. As Susie gave more, she gained more. What she gained was knowledge, which was a good trade off to the young girl. You couldn't put a price on what she had learned. She would give her time, which she had a lot of. She would give her energy, which she could practically bottle up. She would give her love, which sometimes could backfire. The love she would give was taken in many different ways.

Most of the time, the love would become something like a beautiful song. Other times, people would want to keep the song for themselves and not want to share the beautiful tone. When they did, the music would slowly fade way. Susie loved everyone she encountered, and many loved her. That love to her was an inward and outward flow.

The people she had once loved started to betray her. The ones who did not grow started to stop her growth, and darkness would start to surround their lives. They once had a kind glow, but it slowly changed. Her mother warned her of such people that fed on sunshine and drained the water from the earth. Susie never really understood them, but she always stood by waiting for something to happen. As time passed something always did happen. The ones who took and took continued to take some more. So, she could not walk by their side anymore.

Crazy-haired little Susie began to run with the earth. With each sunrise, she would run faster and faster, growing stronger and more graceful. With each sunrise, little Susie would rise, and so would the rest of the earth. She knew she could not take everyone on her entire journey, but those she had to leave behind held a big part of her growth. For that, she was truly thankful.

About the Author

Stacey Ogden is currently a freshman at College of the Desert. This is her first published writing, and she is proud to share them with you. She is planning a life time of learning.

Shadow

Zak O'Mara

"Short stories are tiny windows into other worlds and other minds and dreams. They are journeys you can make to the far side of the universe and still be back in time for dinner."

~Neil Gaiman

Her name is Elizabeth Child. The day was January 10, 2004. Elizabeth was a seventeen-year-old high-school student at Penmen High School, in Los Angeles County, California, and she was going to head to school as usual, but she didn't. There was a mistake. She woke up in her room at 9:45am. If you would have asked her the night before, she would have sworn she had set her alarm. But set or not, it hadn't gone off. So with a start, she leapt out of her bed, got caught in the mangled blue sheets, tripped, fell forward, and caught the top of her dresser to brace herself. The dresser began to tip, and so as to not bring it down with her, she let go of the dresser and resigned herself to the inevitable thud. Elizabeth crashed onto the carpeted floor, hitting her hip first. Her green eyes narrowed at her bed sheets as she kicked the entanglement off her foot. She pursed her lips and, with a furrowed brow and wrinkled nose, nonverbally told the sheets, her bed, and her alarm to go to hell.

She pulled herself up and grabbed her backpack, a small single-sling denim bag containing her books and accessories, and she headed out of her room. She had dressed the night before so as to get an early start that morning and, thus, was already wearing a pink tank top and blue jean shorts. She rushed down the yellow hallway towards the front door, passing by the kitchen. But just as she was pulling on her converse shoes and ready to rush out, she smelled something strange coming from the kitchen. The smell was sweet, very sweet, not unlike the smell of cotton candy. There was a whistling sound coming from the kitchen. Elizabeth crept around the corner to the kitchen, and on the kitchen table, there was a large black mechanical bug. Elizabeth's eyes widened, and she froze in place. The beetle was the source of the whistling noise, as sweet smelling steam shot from the pores in its back.

The machine clicked and turned towards Elizabeth, fixing its large red compound eyes on her. She could see her freckled face reflected in those eyes. The whistling grew louder; then, the beetle jumped up. Elizabeth jumped away to the next room for cover as the mechanical bug exploded. The eggshell tile was stripped off the kitchen floor, the wooden table was splintered, and the floral wallpaper was shredded by the debris. The force of the blast missed Elizabeth as she hit the floor in the living room, but the sound reached her, and for a moment, she could hear absolutely nothing. She pushed herself up on her palms, disoriented by the concussion of the explosive force. She shook her head to clear it and stood up, dizzily.

At that moment a man fell through the roof of her house and landed in the living room. The man did not crash through; in fact, he seemed rather unperturbed by the whole ordeal and landed, still-legged, in front of Elizabeth. The man was about thirty, wore a black suit and dark sunglasses. He left a hole in the roof above him, but were it not for that, it would have appeared as if he had entered the room by the door. "Elizabeth Child," said the intruder. The man reached for Elizabeth and grabbed her arm. "I do apologize, but you will have to come with me," the man said.

Elizabeth hiked up her right leg and kicked the man in the stomach as hard as she could, and that was hard enough. The man was sent flying backwards across the room, and he bashed into the opposite wall. Elizabeth turned away to run out of her house, but before she could exit, the man pulled a gun from his suit and shot a dart into the back of Elizabeth's neck. She yelped as she ran out of her house, down the front yard path and out to the street. She pulled the dart out of the back of her neck and saw what it was: ACID 6. The agent had found her, and marked her with ACID 6. It was only a matter of time now before Elizabeth Child changed back into a shadow.

Elizabeth ran from her home as fast as her legs could carry her. She ran past the suburban households. Each house was a factory built unoriginal box, denoted only by its color. She needed to find a hidden place where she could assess the damage of the ACID 6 without being found by the agent. She needed somewhere to hide, and she knew of only one friend who might be home at that time of day and would help her.

The sun was high in the sky and shone brightly enough to be oppressive to anyone unfortunate enough to be bombarded by its rays. Elizabeth was unfortunate enough to be running in this heat. On a normal day, she would have called her friend Billy to come pick her up, but her phone was in her backpack, and she had dropped that in the living room of her house. She hadn't realized just how far three miles was until that moment, having to walk the distance from her house to Billy's.

High above Elizabeth was a round drone. The drone hovered high in the sky, too high up to be seen by the naked eye. It stared at Elizabeth. The orb had a number of antennae sticking out of the top of its steel chassis. With its central eye, a red lens, it tracked and targeted Elizabeth, relaying her position to the agent.

Elizabeth's lips were chapped, and her body was sweaty. Her jog had slowed down to a trudge as fatigue overcame her. She reached behind her and felt were the dart had struck her. The texture of her skin around the prick had changed, it was smooth like marble. Panicked, Elizabeth tried to quicken her pace. *I will fix this*, she thought. *I have to fix this. Everything will go back to normal.*

The concrete of the sidewalk behind her cracked, and she turned around to see the agent had landed behind her. Unperturbed by his fall, and the cratered cement around him, the agent began to walk towards Elizabeth. She looked around her and saw a home to her left, a shiny blue Jeep to her right. The agent pulled a metal wand from his jacket. The end of the baton fizzled and sparked as he marched towards the girl.

Elizabeth hobbled around to the front of the jeep and grabbed the front bumper. The heat of the sun had left the bumper hot enough to sear her hands. As sweat dripped from her brow, her eyes darted back and forth from the car to the agent. She pulled the car up and strained. The metal bumper blistered her hands as she swung the vehicle around and Frisbee'd the Jeep at the agent. The Jeep crashed, rolled, and vaulted. The twisted metal slammed against the agent and carried him and the wreckage into the nearby house, shattering its white picket fence and tearing out the manicured lawn.

Elizabeth stared at the wreckage for a moment. She slumped and cringed. She had pulled something around her stomach when she threw the car. She resisted the urge to hold her belly since the skin on her palms had been melted raw. Eyes teary, focus wavering and with a stitch in her side, Elizabeth limped on to Billy's house.

Knock! Knock! Knock! Elizabeth rapped on the pastel blue door of Billy's house. There was no answer. She knocked harder, still no answer. "Hello!" She called, still receiving no response. She brought herself to push the doorbell through the stinging of her hands. It didn't work. She knocked yet again to no avail. At last, she tried the handle and found it was locked.

Elizabeth clenched her jaw in frustration. She backed up five steps and turned her shoulder to the door. She charged and kicked off the ground as hard as she could, crashing through the door, pulling it out of its hinges, and bruising her shoulder. She hurried into the house. She had been counting of Billy being there, but for once she needed him around and he wasn't there.

Elizabeth ran to the bathroom to assess the damage. She searched through the cabinets in a frenzy until she found bandages. She wrapped her hands as best as she could and still be able to move her fingers. She sat upon the fake marble counter beside the sink and put her back towards the mirror. She brushed her long blond ponytail out of the way and craned her neck to see the mark left by the dart, and there it was. The skin around the point of impact had turned a shiny black. As Elizabeth watched, to her horror, the mark slowly was expanding down her back and up her neck. She was exposed, and there was no going on as Elizabeth Child. She thought of her mother and her father and of all of the friends she had made in this life. Now, she would have to go.

There was a clicking sound outside of the bathroom door, footsteps, belonging to the agent. She could hear the sounds of whistling coming from more mechanical bugs. She stepped back against the opposite wall, almost tripping into the bathtub. The bathroom door opened and there was the agent, still standing tall, unimpeded, without a mark on his suit. Hovering behind him were three of the beetles. The agent took off his sunglasses.

"Ms. Child." He said. "I am with the ĐYC; you're under arrest for impersonating a human. You will be coming with me to a secure facility wherein you will receive further questioning."

"Why?" Elizabeth spat. "Why do you have to come here and ruin everything? I didn't do anything wrong! I was a good person..." The agent reached out to Elizabeth and smiled a weak, fake smile. The toxin in the dart was seeping through Elizabeth's blood and turning her back into her natural form. She could see in the mirror out of the corner of her eyes that her freckles were disappearing as her skin changed into a blue almost as dark as night. Her eyes grew larger and turned black.

"I was a good human." Elizabeth choked on the words.

Behind her the bathroom wall and ceiling were torn away. Air blasted through and sent the agent and the bugs flying back. Elizabeth remained immobile, standing stiffly against the barrage of wind as the last of her blonde hair turned black.

Hovering above the bathroom was a large aircraft, shaped not unlike a disc. The agent stood up and the machine-bugs shook off the explosion. Elizabeth turned around to face the ship.

"I need to go home now," she said as her mouth faded away. "But, I will be back again someday."

The last the agent saw of Elizabeth Child was a tear she shed before a vacuum-like force sucked her into the aircraft, which then disappeared.

"Agent," a voice in the agent's ear inquired. "Has the shadow been apprehended?"

"I'm afraid not," said the agent, looking out into the distance "But, it'll be back."

About the Author

Zak O'Mara was born in Albuquerque, New Mexico and raised across the United Sates, from Georgia to Nevada. His stories are majorly fantasies and fairytales, pulling from his long-time adoration fables while growing up. He currently lives in California and works as a playwright and a writer of short stories.

Dr. Cassundra White-Elliott

Hiking to the Peak

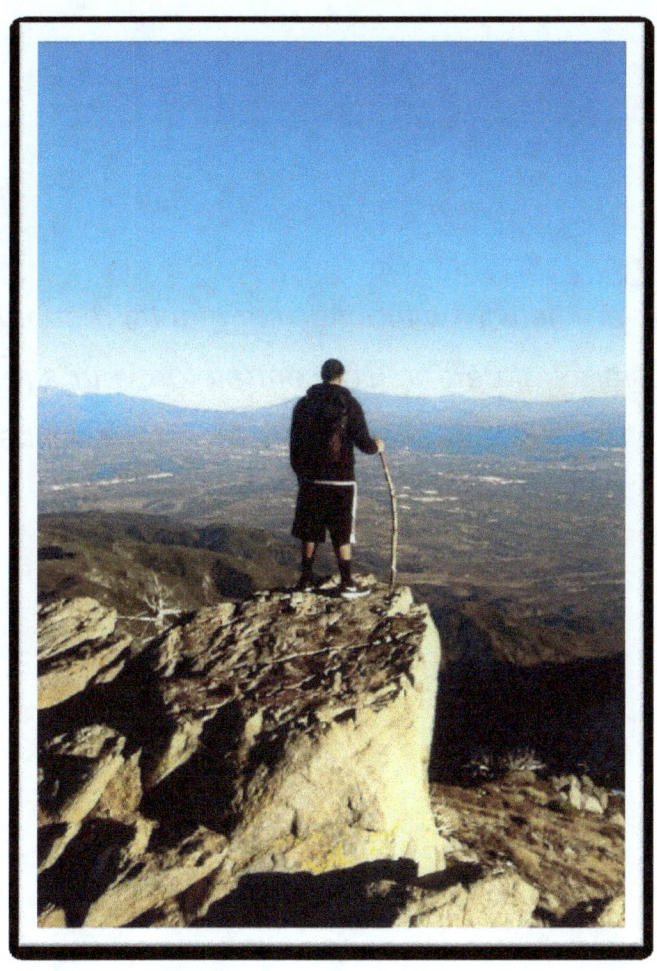

Jason Quezada

"Enter every activity without giving mental recognition to the possibility of defeat. Concentrate on your strengths, instead of your weaknesses… on your powers, instead of your problems."

~Paul J. Meyer

On December 22, 2013, two of my friends and I hiked up to Cucamonga Peak. It was early in the morning around 10am, which is early for me. My friend Leroy gave me a call to ask me if I was ready to go hiking. Leroy has been one of my good friends for many years, fifteen to be exact. He is Black and Puerto Rican, about 6 feet 2 inches tall, and probably weighs about 175-185 pounds. Leroy was already with another one of my friends named Tito. Tito's real name is Alberto, but Tito is what his family has always called him, so it kind of stuck with me as well. He is White and Mexican, but he looks like a white boy because he has light skin. He is about 5 feet 11 inches tall and weighs about 180-190 pounds. Both Leroy and Tito were insisting I go with them on the hike. I remember making plans to do the hike, but a specific date was never agreed on. They just woke up and decided to go on that random morning.

I was extremely tired from the night before. I stayed up really late hanging out with a few coworkers after we got off work. I wasn't really in the mood for a hike. All I wanted to do was sleep some more. After a couple minutes on the phone with Leroy, I decided I would just go on the hike with them.

I quickly got up and started to get dressed for the hike. I wore basketball shorts, a t-shirt (from the 2013 Camp Pendleton Mud run that I had done earlier that year) Nike cross trainers, and a Monster energy drink jacket. Leroy had advised me to put on pants because there would be snow in the mountains, but I wanted to wear shorts, so I could be more agile. The hiking trail we were going on was in Mt. Baldy, a mountain that is fairly close to where we live.

Before we headed to the mountain, we stopped at a gas station to buy water and trail mix for the journey. I had got a Payday candy bar because I did not eat breakfast, and I wanted something in my stomach for the hike. My friend Tito was the only one that was fully prepared for the hike. He brought a sandwich, three small oranges and a banana. Leroy and I should have done the same, but we had no idea what we were in for on this hike. Once we got there, we got all our things together and began our long hike to the top of the Peak.

The hike to Cucamonga Peak was an 11.6 mile hike round trip climbing up 4,300ft of elevation to a peak that stands 8,859ft tall. I had once done an 11.2 mile hike, so I felt confident to do that one. The trail started off smooth, and there were a few other people hiking as well. Mt. Baldy offers many hiking trails, some being easy and others being tough. Of course, we were going on one of the tougher trails, but it did not bother us because we enjoy challenging ourselves. As we started walking up the trail, we were fascinated by the scenery that nature was offering us. There were so many trees. I am no tree expert, but there was a bunch of different kinds. There were a bunch of bushes and shrubs and a ton of rocks everywhere. There was also a little stream of water flowing down the mountain. We came across a few cabins on the hike. Some were still in use, and others were destroyed, and only the foundation and the chimney were still present.

As we continued hiking up the trail, it started to get tougher because the trail started to become steeper. The number of people that we had seen started to drop the more we kept hiking up. Occasionally, we would see a hiker or two coming down the trail. They were dressed as experienced hikers wearing hiking boots, carrying hiking gear and even walking sticks.

At one point, we stopped to ask a guy for directions how to get to the Peak. The look he had on his face when he saw I was in basketball shorts was priceless. He warned us that there was a lot of snow and ice up ahead. He gave us a map of the trail, which showed how to get to our destination. We had already started to see patches of snow about a mile or two up the hike, but once we passed the halfway point of the trail, the snow started to get a little higher than ankle deep. The trail started to become difficult because it had snow and ice covering it. We were constantly slipping and sliding just walking on the trail, and we even fell a few times. It was in that moment that I realized I was completely underdressed, and I should have listened to Leroy's advice about wearing pants.

After passing the halfway point, it was crazy how much harder the hike became. I cannot lie; a few times I wanted to quit and turn back because the pain in my legs was excruciating. The steep incline of the mountain, the cold, and the snow were killing me. I was not the only one having problems with the hike. Leroy was on the same page as I was, but it looked as though he was having a tougher time with it. He had become silent and had a look on his face as if he just wanted to get to the top already. Tito was having a tough time as well but not like Leroy and I.

At one point, Tito went ahead because the trail had ended due to all the snow on the ground. All we heard was him yelling and saying, "Hurry up. You guys have to see this view!" Leroy and I sucked up the pain, and with the last burst of energy we could build up, we sprinted to the top where we heard Tito's voice come from. Once we were there, we were left speechless.

Finally at the top, we were looking down at the whole San Bernardino County, parts of Riverside County, parts of LA County, and much more. It was ridiculous how clear it was and how far we were able to see. Right away, we spotted our houses and the city of Rialto where we lived. My whole life, I had been able to see that mountain peak from my house, and there I was looking down at my house from the top of the peak. Words could not fully describe the beauty that place had to offer. It felt as if all our problems and worries went away for that brief moment we were up there.

The sun was already starting to set. So, we were lucky enough to witness the beauty of the Southern California sunset from up there. All three of us sat on the edge of a rock that had at least a 20ft drop or more on it. We just admired the view and all that the peak had to offer.

It's not every day that a random adventure with your friends turns into something that you will remember for the rest of your life.

About the Author

Jason Quezada is twenty-two years old. He grew up in Rialto, CA. He started attending Crafton Hills College in fall of 2014 to pursue a career in the fire service. At Crafton, he was taking an English class and learned of an opportunity to participate in publishing a compilation of short stories. Participating in the publishing sounded rather interesting to him, and he felt it would be a great experience to have a book published with a story of his in it. He was right about the experience and may consider publishing another story in the future.

Fifty-One-Fifty

Kayghee Reynolds

"I have shed so many tears

For all my failures

And I'm all dried out"

~Kayghee Reynolds

A cold sweat broke out over Heather's face as she sat in the tiny dilapidated room and listened to her mother, Cindy, argue with the doctors. Cindy was a dark-skinned Latina, with thick coarse black hair that curled all the way down to her mid-back. Heather, with her pale skin and hazel eyes, obviously didn't inherit much of her mother's coloring. She got her looks from her Scottish father, along with his height. He was not there, because he had to take care of the house and make sure her younger brother, Brad, got to school. Heather didn't mean to become such a burden on her family. Honestly, she hadn't planned on being anything. She had swallowed countless pills and alcohol in an attempt to cease to exist. Giving up always seemed very tempting to Heather, but it became the only answer when school, a broken heart, and one too many deaths in the family finally became too much. This all led to this small room with the broken ceiling tiles and dirty walls. It was the reason her mom questioned why she had to be here.

"It is mandatory for people like her to be put on a 72-hour watch," said the man sitting behind the desk.

"But why does she need to stay here? Is there no place else?" Cindy's furrowed brow and disgusted pout gave away how truly uncomfortable she was leaving her only daughter in such a place.

"Ma'am, we are the only outpatient facility with a youth ward in Orange County. If you do not have her voluntarily put in here, we will be forced to make her stay, and it will end up on her record for life." The doctor kept his stern eyes on Heather the entire time.

Cindy knew there was nothing she could do, so she had her daughter's possessions checked in at the front. Heather watched silently as her stuff was poked and prodded. Then, her bear came out of the bag. It was a cute bear with light tan fur, a pink nose, and a bow to match.

"Either, we cut off the ribbon, or you can't have the bear with you," the bulky stoic orderly stated.

"But... why?" Heather loved how sweet the bow made her bear look and helped add to the irony of its name, Killer.

"It can be used as a weapon and as a way to hang yourself, so it has to go." The scissors in his hands seemed to shine menacingly as he spoke. Heather nodded to cut the ribbon and felt her privacy cut away with it.

Cindy kissed and hugged Heather good bye and was escorted away. Another orderly came and grabbed the approved items she had brought and walked her to her shared room. The four walls were a startling white. One had a small window that looked into the play area and another wall had the entrance with no door. The policy of no doors was so patients could either off themselves or anyone else. The only room where patients were allowed to be alone and have a door was the shower/bathroom, but there were no locks. Heather put what she had either on the bed or into the drawer she was given that was under her nightstand. The orderly stood in the entrance way until she was done unpacking. Heather turned to the short woman and informed her she was done. The woman waived for Heather to follow, and they began a rather short tour of the tiny wing that would be her home for the next three days.

"This is the main room. You'll have down time in here, class, group therapy session and in the back room is where you'll have your one-on-one session with the doctor. My name is Rose. If you need anything, just come see us at the desk. Don't go outside or into your room unless instructed, and you need to ask us to escort you to the bathroom." The orderly told Heather to mingle with the other patients and bobbed away.

There were five other people scattered in the room: two boys and three girls, all between the ages of 14-17. Over at the table talking, there was a shy young girl with long brown hair, a black hoodie, and a look of dread. She was being talked at and she didn't seem to be responding back to a boy with scraggly hair and a look that makes you question if he belonged to the wing next door with the permanent residences. On the couch was a large boy laughing at a movie with a long-legged girl who almost snorted the water out of her nose that she was drinking. Heather pulled up a chair at a different table and faced the TV. It looked like they were watching Benchwarmers and were about halfway through. Heather had seen the movie a million times. So, instead, she focused her attention on the couch. It was "L" shaped, made of a leather that was an unattractive dark green color and looked like it had seen the end of World War II.

"Hello!" A curvy girl plopped down in front of Heather and interrupted her analysis of that ugly old couch.

"Um... Hello."

"My name is Shandra! I've been here since yesterday. I basically know everything there needs to be known about this place. I saw you had family bring you. That's nice. My family didn't find out 'til this morning. They kinda suck. Did your mom put you in her because she didn't wanna deal with you or what? You don't look like the crazy type or really the drug type. Why are you here?" She almost didn't take a breath during her whole introduction.

Heather blinked deliberately and slowly as she tried to decipher what Shandra had just said. "Uh... no. My family didn't really put me in here. I did it when I tried to kill myself with a handful of pills."

"Me too!" Spit flew out of her mouth, luckily missing Heather completely. "I tried to off myself by overdosing on meth, but that obviously didn't work out. I am tired of my fucking family. Wanna see a picture of my baby? Look..." She pulled out a black and white wrinkled picture from her pocket. "See? He's got my hair, but he's got my daddy's eyes. Yeah, that's my daddy's baby, but Momma won't believe me. She says I'm a liar. So, I left and tried to kill myself, but I sure do miss my baby. I love that baby more than I love me!"

Shandra rambled on 'til two orderlies walked in with a large collection of trays and announced lunchtime. Every gray tray had a little piece of paper with a name and any dietary accommodations scribbled at the very bottom. Heather remembered filling out paperwork earlier stating she was a vegetarian. When she got her plate and opened it up, there was a simple salad and a PB&J sandwich. She sat at the table where everyone else had already started working on their meals. The girl who was sitting there earlier still hadn't gotten up to get her plate. The bulky orderly from before came over.

"Sara, you need to come grab your plate." He waited for any signs of life. "Please."

Her eyes shifted to the cart, and she got up slowly. Her hair seemed to move on its own when she walked, and her arms did not swing, which was very unnerving and beautiful. When she sat back down with her tray, Heather's stare was met with her black eyes. Heather glanced away quickly and locked eyes with the boy who was talking to Sara earlier, now on the opposite side of the table.

"Hello, my name is Hank. His gentle beast is George. I saw you meet Shandra earlier. That's Sara, and finally, this is Miss Charlotte. What is your name, Madame?" Heather gagged on how sweet his voice was.

"My name is Heather. Nice to meet you all officially." She actually hated meeting new people. It was painful to make small talk and pretend to care about what people have to say.

"Hi, Heather. I hope you don't mind me asking, but why are you here?" George had a deep rich voice that really needed only to be above a whisper to hear.

"I don't mind. I tried to commit suicide by swallowing a handful of pills. I was at the hospital for three days, and now, I am here for another three." Her story was one she didn't mind sharing. Her life was an open book; but one only needed to ask.

"I think most of us are in here for that, except for Charlotte. She tried to stab someone when she took a shot of heroine, but she's cool now. I am leaving tonight actually; just got done with my three-day hold and am waiting on my parents to show up." Hank smiled like he won a triathlon as he said the last sentence. He did have something to be proud of.

As the group continued to talk, Heather learned a little bit more about each of them. Hank tried killing himself because of the pressure to be perfect at sports, school and life in general. When his parents showed up yesterday to visit, he explained the mounting pressure he felt from them. They all cried and hugged it out; his parents had no idea they were doing that to him and promised to be better. They told him how at sixteen, they shouldn't put that much weight on his shoulders. Charlotte had some anger issues that ended with her trying to stab a friend at school because her friend won a game of handball. She was the youngest of all, at the age of fourteen. She had a lot of issues with controlling her emotions in general and told the group how that wasn't exactly her first time in a psych hold. George tried hanging himself. The bullying and name calling from being a larger guy was too much for his sweet heart to handle. Similarly, his weight was too much for the rope and fan to handle, which is why his grandma found him.

The group continued talking, except Sara. She hadn't said a word the whole time, and before Heather could ask her any questions, they called the group together for a group therapy session. They all gathered the chairs in a circle and waited. Hank grabbed an extra for the therapist who was arriving shortly. When she entered the room, Heather was intrigued because of her clothing. She was wearing jeans, a regular t-shirt and a blazer. Her hair was in a messy ponytail, and her glasses were rimless. Everyone stayed quiet as she got settled into her spot and opened her black soft leather brief case.

"Hello, everyone. I see we have a new face! My name is Stephanie Gunderson. You may call me Dr. Gunderson. What is your name and can you tell us a little about yourself?" That question came up a lot that day, and Heather honestly thought about wearing a nametag to prevent it from coming up again.

"Hello, my name is Heather. I am a seventeen-year-old senior at Sonora High School. I play the trumpet in band, and I am chronically depressed." She made her voice sound like she was at an AA meeting.

"Thank you, Miss Heather. Today's activity is about your inner bully. I'm going to pass out this story and have you all read it to yourself." Dr. Gunderson passed out the papers and waited as they all sat quietly and read it internally. Once all of their heads popped up again, she explained the assignment.

"In this story, you learn about a girl who is beaten and bullied by someone who is following her around. By the end, you come to find out that her bully was her internal voice the whole time. I am passing around another piece of paper. This time it is blank. I would like you to take a pen and write down three things your inner bully tells you. When you are done, please put your pen down." This time, instead of waiting, Dr. Gunderson pulled out her own pen and wrote down her own list of three. Heather scribbled down her list: I am dumb, I am not good enough, and I am unimportant.

"Now that everyone is done writing down their list, I want you to pick a buddy and swap papers. There is an odd number. So, Heather, I would like to swap with you, and you can swap my paper with someone else." Dr. Gunderson hands Heather her paper, and Heather gave the doctor hers.

"Okay, everyone have someone else's? Good. What I would like everyone to do is say those things to the person who wrote them like you are the inner voice. Ready?" Dr. Gunderson faced Heather and began repeating the list back to her.

"You fail at everything, you are dumb, you are not good enough, and you are unimportant." Heather felt tears in her eyes hearing those things being said aloud.

"Alright, everyone. Bring it back. My question for everyone is how did that make you feel? Would you ever let someone talk to you like that?" Everyone shook their head. "Wouldn't you want to kick that person's ass?" This time people nodded and grunted in agreement. "So why is it… that it's okay for you to say that to yourself?" The group sat quietly, most of them still reeling from that mind-blowing revelation.

"Your next task is to write down something positive based off the list of the other person. Please put your pen down when you are done." Again, everyone looked down and scribbled away. Heather tried doing her best, but positive spins were not her thing. "Now, please read what you wrote to the other person." Dr. Gunderson faced Heather and said, "You do great just the way you are. You are brilliant, you are good enough, and you are so special."

Heather's eyes welled up, and her mind drifted off. She had only ever been so mean and abusive to herself. In the story, the girl gave her inner voice a name. It was the name of someone who had tormented her for years. So who would hers be? For the longest time, she blamed her mother, but her mother was so loving and encouraging that the title of bully did not fit her. Thinking back deep into her mind, she remembered living with a girl named Lauren, who was a nasty thing that always told her things like, remember to suck in your belly so you don't look so fat and no one wants to be your friend. Lauren was the voice of her inner bully, and Heather planned on kicking her out.

"That will be all. Have a wonderful rest of the day." Dr. Gunderson said as she packed her things, then left.

About the same time she exited, the orderlies, the bulky male and the tiny female from earlier, entered the room with the cart of trays. Everyone moved their chairs back to where they belonged and got in line for food, all except Hank, who had basically burst out of the room when he saw his parents at the desk filling out the final paper work to release him. He came back and hugged them all; then, he left to pack his things. Sara was a little bit more proactive in getting her food and actually giggled when Heather tripped and nearly threw her food everywhere. Once they were all seated, they talked about what they had learned in group.

"Fuck my inner bully, man! I'd kill her if I could!" Charlotte spat out in between chewing her Salisbury steak.

"I really liked the exercise! It helped me better understand what I say in my mind isn't truth! When I get home, I'm gonna tell my momma and daddy and my baby! My baby won't really understand but hopefully he'll internalize it and he'll be better for it. I know there is stuff we live our lives by that we don't even remember and the same will go for my baby. Mhm, he won't remember me telling him, but I would have said it, so that's all that matters!" Heather was impressed by Shandra's ability to speak and eat. She should become one of those people that works at auctions and sells the items.

"I think I got a lot out of it. If I can stop my inner bully, maybe the outer bully's words won't hurt so much." George hadn't even touched his food yet, but he was pretty good about waiting between forkfuls to say something.

"Me too. What about you, Sara?" Heather wanted to get her involved.

"Eh. It was cool." Sara's voice was very monotone but still captured the attention of everyone around her.

Once dinner and the conversation were done, the patients were allowed to hang out or take a shower before bed. Heather was one for morning showers, so she walked over to the tall long desk and talked to Mr. Bulky.

"Hello."

"Hello, ma'am. What can I do for you?"

"I just kind of want to talk." She looked at his name badge and saw it said Eric.

"Oh, okay. How are you today? Heather right?"

"I'm alright, could be better, and yes, it's Heather. I miss having paper and pens to draw."

"You like drawing? Me too. I do more graffiti art though. I can't get you a pen but we have paper and crayons for you guys."

"I do and would love a crayon or two. Can you draw me something?"

"Alright, follow me." He got up and had her follow him to the main room. "I can draw you something. Like what?"

"My name would be a cool thing." He showed her where the plastic bin was that held all of the art supplies; it was very similar to a kindergarten class, minus the scissors. "Thanks!"

"Not a problem, and consider it done!"

Eric left Heather to doodle, which she did for a long while before it was lights out. When it was time for bed, Heather cleaned up the mess she made and walked to her room. It turned out her roommate was Sara. She had just taken a shower and was combing her hair when Heather came in.

"Sara, can I ask why you are in here?"

"Similar reasons to you. Just a different method." Sara flashed her two rather large barely healing scars on her arms. "They found me in my room. My boy scout of a brother kept me from bleeding out 'til the paramedics showed up."

"Wow, was it your first time?"

"This is my third time in here in a month. My new tactic is to stop eating, but that's a hard one to do."

Sara and Heather talked most of the night about their stories 'til Eric had to finally come in and hush them up. Though she felt very alone and scared when she showed up, Heather actually felt more connected to other human beings than she ever had before. The black room around her welcomed her sleepy eyes to shut as she thought of that and her new much more positive look on the future before her.

About the Author

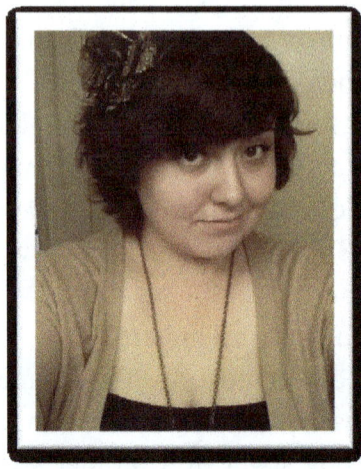

Kayghee has been writing for eleven years, but this is her first short story. Her main love can is poetry, because she likes to get her ideas out in as few words as possible. Kayghee grew up in small town La Habra, CA and graduated from one of the high schools. While there, she joined the band and a medical academy to start a career in the medical field. After her four years in the program were up, she decided she wanted to actually study psychology. This led her to Fullerton College where she has been taking her classes for general education and for her psychology major.

Outside of school, she is heavily involved with the Boy Scouts of America as an adult leader in a troop, crew and OA chapter. She herself has gone through the program and earned the Silver award in her crew. Along with scouting, she likes to spend her spare time painting, hanging out with her friends and reading. She hopes to one day make a career out of her art and writing.

A Touch of Paradise

Gary Rodriguez

"Is this safe?" I ask my friend as we try to navigate a safe path to descend the ridge we are on.

"Sure, I know these mountains like the back of my hand," the man says.

"Good. I don't think I could climb down the way the others did with this guitar case in my hand." Then, just as soon as he assures me it was safe… Crash! Whack! The dust and ash fly, as two guys tumble and slide down a fire-stricken slope in an avalanche fashion. As we tumble, I hold onto my guitar case for dear life, as I crash into several charred trees in the area. After hitting the bottom, I say to myself, *Where's my guitar case?* Click, click. My friend turns his head to the direction of the clicking sound.

"Watch out!" he tries to motion to me with a panicked look on his face. As he looks helplessly, I immediately recall that my guitar case is no longer in my hand. Then as if by an angel's divine protective instinct, I thrust my right arm backwards catching the twenty-pound hardwood guitar case like a football quarterback in the process of releasing the ball. And, after briefly catching it, I guide the guitar case a solid ten feet in front of me. All this occurred in under a minute. Still filled with adrenaline, I try to get ahold of myself.

Then, after taking a few breaths, I look at my friend to gain confirmation that he is all right. My friend is a tall lengthy man of about six feet. He has brown hair, dark brown eyes, and is covered in sand and ash from the fall.

"Thanks for the warning, Rob," I say. Rob gives a quick glance over at me seeing that I too am covered in ash and sand.

"You all right, Gary?" he laughs for a second and thinks to himself, *Of course, he is. I mean he's built like a football player.* After laughing at our helplessness, he stands up. I myself still covered in sand and ash begin to stand up and shake the dirt out of my dark brown hair. As I position myself, I lean forward reaching my hands into the dirt before me to notice that it is very soft. While getting up I ponder to myself, *Why is the dirt was soft like sand?*

Once up, I turn around to see the dust cloud slowly rise and dissipate. Then, as if the moon wants to illuminate our path, the clouds depart from the moon bringing light to our surroundings. We look up towards our previous position. This makes us realize why what had occurred had occurred. Ash and charred trees filled the side of the hill from where we had fallen.

Being flabbergasted and bamboozled, we retrace our steps. Climbing up the hill, I notice which path I had fallen from. I am confident to say the least, because there is a trail of busted and broken tree branches everywhere. The destructive scene was caused by my guitar case while it was in my hand. After carefully analyzing the scene of the fall, we look at each other and conclude what happened. There before us, on the ground, was a giant rock, which had crumbled into two. While on the ridge, we figured that the rock was not charred.

"It must have been weak from the fire three months ago," he said. Feeling lucky, we joke that death had dumped me and cancelled our date that night. We then proceed to meet with our other friends who had been on their way to the meeting point. As we proceed on to our rendezvous point with the group, I close my eyes to remember just how I got here.

It was ten o'clock in the morning and summer vacation. Like all young guys my age, I was sleeping. I had nothing to do, nothing planned, and expected nothing eventful to happen. While I slept, however, others were not thinking the way I was. "Guess who just got back today? Those wild-eyed boys that had been away haven't changed, haven't much to say. But man, I still think those cats are great" (The ringtone is playing the song of the Thin Lizzy's "The Boys Are Back in Town"). By the time the song finished that line, I had awakened.

I rustled out of the thin white sheets that were on my bed and reached for my cell, which was on my dresser. "Hello?" I answered with a deep baritone voice, crust in my eyes and a hairstyle that looked like I came out of a tornado.

"Gary!" The voice answered back. "I have a proposition for you." I lifted my head with my eyes half opened and said, "Well, since you've disturbed me from my hibernation, I might as well hear you out."

The voice continued and said, "I just got the okay from my mom to take you, me, Rich, Mendez, and Chris up to Porter Ranch for the week. Can you go?" At that point, I looked up at my screen to see whom I was speaking to. The screen read Rob Salazar. *Figures as much coming from Rob,* I said to myself.

"What time are we meeting and where?" I asked him.

"We will meet up at Rich's house at 14 hundred hours."

"Sounds good," I replied. The phone call ended and left me curious. What could Rob have planned that could take up a whole week and on top of all that at his mom's place? Getting out of bed, I chuckled to myself at the very idea that whatever he had planned it must be crazy. He's pretty smart, too smart for his own good sometimes. It's kind of funny. Aside from his intelligence, he also possesses the necessary skills to be an outstanding leader. Actually, everyone in this group possessed similar traits, which is probably the reason why we all get along well.

After pondering the numerous events that may take place, I sprung myself from the bed and began to gather all the materials needed for the trip. I filled my duffle bag up to bursting with clothes, hygienic materials, and medication. Then, another thought hit me. I'm getting ready to embark on this journey, and I haven't even told my folks yet. How are they going to react to my sudden leave of absence? I come from a family that likes parental control, even though I am adult by age. And from past experience, I've learned that they like to be in charge of when I departed and returned. Their control doesn't sit well with me though, as I am a free-spirited kind of guy. So, I shall tell them on my way out the door.

One thirty rolled around, and the doorbell rang. I told my parents I'd be gone for a week, and my ride was already outside. They weren't too pleased, but they also never like to keep others waiting.

I know I'll hear it later, but I'll handle that problem when I reach it. As I walked out, I greeted my friend Chris. Chris is about as tall as I am at about five eleven, looks kinda Indian with his Moreno-colored skin, has dark brown eyes, long black hair, and has the athletic build of a runner. After we greeted one another with a signature handshake, I realized I didn't have my guitar.

"We can't have good road trip without music. Can we?" I said to Chris.

"Nope, unless you want us to be extremely bored out of our freakin' minds up there," he said very sarcastically. Chris is also a musician like me; I know he understood my needs. After grabbing my black Yamaha guitar case, we left in his van.

As we pulled up to Rich's house, we saw our crew of friends grabbing their supplies and shoving them into a Jeep. It had been awhile since the crew last got together, maybe three months at the least. As we gather our stuff from the van, we yell, "Mendez! As he turned around, we notice his gear is stacked higher than he is.

"Little high, little low," I yelled to Mendez, but only to receive a spiteful, "Shut up" and a middle finger. Mendez is a short guy about five seven in height, kinda nerdy looking, clean cut, with black hair and eyes. Running out of the house was Rich yelling, "Hurry up. We're on a time limit, guys. And, we don't want to keep our ride waiting." He is about as tall as Chris and I, a ginger kid, red hair, blue eyes, clean cut and built like a runner. He never likes to be late, so he helped us pack the last of our supplies into the Jeep.

"Umm, how are all gonna fit inside the car with all this stuff?" I asked.

"Well, two people are going to have to sit in the trunk with all the stuff. Just duck your heads if you see the police," Rob said.

"I vote Chris and Mendez!" Rich yells. Then, they look to me.

"I ain't going back there. I'm too big," I said.

"Well, on the way back one of you's is gonna sit in the trunk," Chris said. Laughing at Chris, Mendez said, "I'm short and can fit like a contortionist." With that being settled, Chris and Mendez sat in the trunk. After we settled ourselves in like Tetris blocks, Rob introduced us to his mom and sister. He then also went on to talk about how he and Rich had been planning the trip for a couple of days but barely decided to inform us a couple of hours prior to our trip.

After everything was said and settled, we departed for Porter Ranch to spend our week. The car ride was pretty boring and offered little excitement. However, it was a bit funny when Chris and Mendez would hide from California Highway Patrol officers every time one was spotted. Altogether, the ride last a little over three hours. When we finally reached our destination, everyone except for Rob, his mom, and his sister were in shock. What we saw was an isolated area with a full security staff on post and nice beautiful houses everywhere.

At that point, we knew Rob's mom had money. After rounding the corner, we pulled into the driveway and unpacked ourselves. We were like stuffed sardines packed tightly. Well, everyone except for Chris and Mendez. They were packed in the trunk like an over-filled closet ready to explode. I jokingly said to them, "Are you ready to be released from your eternal imprisonment?!"

"YES!" they chorused, as I laughed and pulled the lever of their freedom. The trio of Rob, Rich, and myself burst into a thunderous laughter with tears trailing down our faces. Then, looking down at our stiff legs, we laughed some more. By that time, Chris and Mendez got out of the car very awkwardly; their legs had gone into a deep slumber. As they stood up, their legs began to tremble like a one-year-old child learning how to walk. Our laughter went from a hysterical funny laugh to a painful laugh, as we held onto our stomachs.

After we finished our laughing, I turned around to see the house. Rob's house was a beautiful two-story house. It had dark green grass, small palm trees stationed at the four corners of the yard, lights all around the driveway, and a running water fountain with an angel on top. After my brief adoration of the house, I gathered my gear and followed the group inside. The inside is like what you'd expect from anybody well off: lots of furniture, beautiful paintings on the walls, a nice kitchen, and a big T.V. with a loud surround sound. After we got inside, we dropped off our stuff off in Rob's room.

"GO CHANGE!" Rob's mom yelled from the kitchen. "WE HAVE A POOL OUTSIDE!" Rob forgot to mention that he had a pool; luckily, I had packed gym shorts just in case. In any event, we all gathered our swimwear and headed outside. By that time, it was about seven in the evening, the weather was fair, and the backyard looked like a scene taken out of a movie, one where there was a small oasis in the middle of nowhere with a small waterfall. After another awe-inspiring view, I turned my attention towards the fence and viewed what lay beyond it. As I approached the fence to see exactly where we were, I was again awe stricken. What I saw was the city of Los Angeles. I could see the big buildings, the street lights, cars driving through the streets; I had never seen L.A. like that before.

Once my experience had ended, I turned around to see Rob's mom and stepdad, and by the looks of things, it was time for introductions. Other than our brief meeting on the ride there, I had paid little attention to what she actually looked like. She was in shape and obviously a woman who took care of herself, had dirty blond hair and dark brown eyes, and was Caucasian like Rob. Her husband Mike was also in shape, rather tall and was African American. Once finished with their introductions, they lay down the rules of their home: "Don't let the children go near the water unsupervised, don't be too loud, you're welcome to feed yourself, and have a good time while you're here." Rob's younger siblings were not there at the time, so that was one thing to mark off for that night.

With that, we all jumped into the pool. I immediately grabbed Chris and submerged him underwater. *That was probably a bad idea,* I thought to myself. Then all of a sudden, Chris gets out from under me and pulls me under. *Crap!* I thought it was definitely a bad idea. I can't swim that well. The rough housing went on for a little while then died off. By that time, it was around 7:45. We were in paradise. I felt really free and safe, and it was my assumption that we'd stay there the rest of the night, but I was about to be proven otherwise. 8:30 rolled around, and we had made our way to the Jacuzzi waterfall. We sat there and just soaked up the heat. It was a nice change and very relaxing.

"So, there are mountains near here that I've been exploring, and I know the perfect spot to camp," Rob says. We look around at each other and thought to ourselves, *Rob has never done anything that was an extremely bad idea, except maybe when he convinced us to ditch in high school. That almost got us caught by the police.*

"Sure, why not!" we replied. With our decisions made, we got out and dressed for the soon to come event. *A list,* I thought.

"What do we need, Rob?" I asked.

"Well, since it will only take about 20 minutes to get there, we shall take a flashlight, a tent, and one sleeping bag to lie on. It's summer. Who needs to be covered anyways?" He chuckled as he said these things.

I grabbed a few bags of Top Ramen and some waters, just in case. I like to be prepared. Oh, and my trusty guitar. Then came our final obstacle. It was nine o'clock in the evening and there we were, a bunch of young adults, about to embark on a journey in camouflaged gear.

"Where are you all going?" Rob's mom asked.

"We're going in those mountains behind the block to camp," Rob said proudly.

"Don't you know it's unsafe to travel in the mountains?" Rob's mom commented.

I felt that was a good time to jump in, "This might sound crazy, but I can ensure the group's safety." I was the oldest, so it seemed right to do so. After careful consideration, Rob's mom finally gave the okay on the account that we text her upon arrival and our return in the morning, or she would send a search team.

With matters settled, we made our way to the security post. Upon arriving at the post, we got strange looks and a few chuckles from the guards. Looking back, I probably would have laughed at us too. What they saw was a rag tag group of kids who looked like they were dressed to play in a Vietnam War movie, accompanied by a guitarist. As you might have noticed by now we were military geeks, and that felt like a mission, a mission to infiltrate the hills and scout out the area. Without any objections, they let us go.

We must have walked for about ten minutes until we came across an opening near the hills. There was sand and wild life everywhere. Ten minutes passed, and we reached the base of the hill. The hill looked steep and would obviously prove to be a tough climb. At that point in time, small clouds began to cover the moon limiting our light.

"What now, Rob, no light?" Rich and Mendez asked. Rob chuckled at their uncertainty and shaken resolve; then, he pulled out a five-inch LED flashlight.

"Here's your light!" he said while laughing lightly to himself.

"Well, we're already this far, so we might as well keep going," Chris and I said. Waiting to get the approval from Mendez and Rich, we looked back to them, but see they were still a bit uncertain of the small LED flashlight.

"We just have one flashlight, and this doesn't seem to be a good idea," Rich said.

"Nonsense!" Rob said as he turned on the flashlight to prove to us the distance it could illuminate. If I would have to take a guess on the distance, I would estimate anywhere from eight hundred to a thousand feet. With everyone on board, we ascended up the steep hill. Then about 200 feet in, I slipped and fell. And, as I began falling, Rich, who was in front of me, turned around and caught me by my guitar case.

"Whew! That was a close one," Rich said.

"Yeah. Thanks. I would have taken a nasty fall if it weren't for that." After that small incident, we continued the climb with Rob leading the way. We must have climbed that hill for fifteen minutes, until we reached the top. The top was filled with brush and wild trees. Human alteration was nowhere to be seen.

Then out of nowhere, we heard the sound of coyotes howling out in the distant. Thump, thump, I could feel my heart rate start to rise as I looked around to see if any coyotes were near. Snap! Crack! We turned our heads quickly to our right in a desperate effort to locate the sound. Then, after a few seconds of silence, two jack rabbits raced out of the brush chasing each other. Wow! We chorused. All that for a couple of jack rabbits? Our pulses were a little high after that, as we laughed at our frightened selves.

After confirming nothing else was near, we proceeded. The path we took kind of resembled a trail or maybe a dried up stream. Either way, it was a solid path to take uninterrupted by the brush. About five minutes into the walk, we heard the howls again, and due to the hollowness of the hills, the sound bounced off the rocks leaving us unable to determine their location. *The howls brought about a sense of excitement,* I thought to myself as we continued to walk.

"Wait! Stop!" The immediate halt was unexpected and caused us to bump into each other.

"Why did we stop, Rob?" I said from the back of the group. Curiously, I made way to the front of the group. There before me was a cliff with no sign of an end. The darkness made it seem ominous.

"Oh, yeah. I forgot to mention the big drop that was here. I always come in the daytime, so the lighting is never a problem. The drop is only about a hundred feet." Rob laughed. After viewing the fall, Rob pointed to our destination down below about one hundred yards away.

"Great. I bring a guitar, and now I gotta climb this cliff."

"It's easy," Rob exclaimed and handed the light over to Rich who was doubtful. "Shine the light on me as I climb down," Rob said while he descended.

Laughing, Chris and Mendez yell, "You make it look so easy!"

Rob laughing from below, "It is. Your turn, Chris."

"Screw it," Chris said as he descended. After him descended, Mendez followed. Now the only people on the ridge are Rich and I, along with and all of our supplies. Rich, paranoid at the situation he got into began to descend saying, "If I fall, I'm suing all of you!"

"That is if we don't leave you there first!" Mendez yelled and laughed hard with Rob and Chris.

Now it's my turn, I thought. "How the hell am I gonna get down there with my guitar?"

"Toss all the stuff down, including your guitar!" Rob yelled up to me.

"Are you crazy?" Chris and Rich yell. "That thing is heavy!"

Overruled by the majority's decision, Rob climbed back up. "I know another way that might be easier," Rob said.

"Screw you, Rob," Rich yelled. "You could have showed us that way instead." After that, we tossed the supplies to them, excluding my guitar.

"Set up the tent in that sandy area out there," Rob yelled. We then began to walk towards a ridge that was about 90 feet away. As soon as we reached it- Crash! Whack! As I opened my eyes, I am reminded with scattered evidence as to how I finally got here from the fall.

Where would I be had I not picked up my phone this morning? I thought. *I sure as hell wouldn't be here.*

With a moonlit path before us, Rob and I proceeded down the slope. However, we descend safely. After dusting ourselves off, we went to meet up with the guys.

"You're a freakin' idiot, Rob," Rich yelled.

"What? Why?"

"That?!" Knowing why Rich was pointing, he laughed. Curious myself, I looked to the side where Rich was pointing, and I didn't believe what I saw. The entrance we saw on our way up there was our final destination! Ten minutes from where Rob lived was our actual destination. By that time, Rob was laughing hysterically, and it caught like wild fire as we all start dying of laughter.

"Don't be mad. What's the point of taking the easier route? There's no fun involved!" Rob yelled.

"First, you decided on this crazy idea of camping in the mountains. Then, you take us past our destination on purpose, and on top of all that, you almost got me and everyone else killed!" At that point, we burst out in laughter at the dangerous adventure we just embarked on. I look back at Rich with watering eyes to see that he was dumbfounded still. Then, Rich gave in and started laughing at it too saying, "Screw you guys!"

Well, if there's anything I can take from that adventure is taking the easy route may get you to your location quicker, but taking the hard way will give you memories that you'll always remember. Quoting the great American poet Robert Frost, "Two roads diverged in a wood, and I--I took the one less traveled by, and that has made all the difference."

Still, this is only the first night. I wonder what Rob has planned for tomorrow....

About the Author

Gary Rodriguez is a young native of San Bernardino who is currently studying Business Management at the University of Phoenix's San Bernardino Campus. His goals for the next two years include gaining experiences in marketing, writing, and attaining his Bachelor's degree. His passions include singing opera, writing poetry, writing Bach style Chorales, and playing guitar. Gary is also an active musician in the community and often performs with the San Bernardino Valley College Music Department, local community centers, and in his church.

Embrace Every Moment

Karen Ruiz

"Live in the present, launch yourself on every wave, find eternity in each moment."
Henry David Thoreau

Everyone has goals in life, but sadly, not everyone gets to reach his/her potential goals. We live in a society where everyone is too busy working and stressing about things and situations we do not know the outcome that we forget to live a little. I gave myself a goal to live a little, to embrace my surroundings, to adventure and love like there is no tomorrow. At the young age of seventeen, my life changed dramatically.

Growing up, I had no worries. My only obligation was to give my schooling my all and to make sure I could be the best version of myself. I was blessed enough to have parents who would go out of their way for my sisters and me. They didn't attend every meeting at school, but every day I had a home to go to and a meal to eat. I had the best support system any girl could ask for. Everyone that I encountered believed in me and said I was going to be someone great in life. I took those words to the heart, and whenever I was feeling down or doubted myself, I replayed those words in my head.

I remembered all the sacrifices my mom and dad made in order to give my sisters and me the best. All the late nights of crying because I couldn't seem to understand everything in the textbook turned into frustration. But then came along my dad and would continuously say to me, "I came to this country, so I could give you and your sisters what I always desired but my parents couldn't give to me. I work in the heat, so one day you won't have to be in the California summer trying to earn your money."

I had it so easy, and I took everything for granted. I had it picture perfect but never stopped to realize all the blessings I had. Like every family, we had our arguments and our fights, but we always came back together. Until it all came to a flip.

On April 15, 2015, my family and I received one of the worse news possible. My mom was diagnosed with aggressive breast cancer in both her breasts. I will never forget that day. I woke up just like every other day and got ready for school. My older sister, Daisy, was getting ready to go to her morning class, while my dad yelled at me and my baby sister to hurry up or we were going to be late for school. I went throughout my day never thinking we would get bad news. I remember texting my sister asking if my mom's doctor's appointment went well, and she didn't reply.

School was over, and my baby sister and I were waiting for my dad to pick us up from school. We got in the truck, and my dad didn't say one word. I asked him how my mom's appointment went, and he said nothing. We were almost to the house when my dad said, " Your mom doesn't feel good, so don't bug her." I knew something was wrong, but I didn't know what. We finally got home, and I remember walking into the kitchen, and my mom was crying while trying to cook. I went to hug her and cried because I was scared of what words were going to come out her mouth. She said, "The doctors said I have cancer." My world came crashing down.

I always associated cancer with death. I never knew anyone who had cancer. All I knew was that it was a disease that killed people. I didn't know what to do or say other than cry and feel helpless. I had so many questions, and no one to answer them. I just knew I had to be strong for my mom no matter what was coming our way.

A couple of weeks went by, and my parents spoke to specialists about the next steps to fighting this horrible disease. Soon, my mom was given a surgery date which was June 5, 2015. At that time, my dad had to go back to Texas for work, which left my mom, two sisters and me by ourselves. Never did I feel so alone yet so motivated to come out this stronger than ever.

But, I was mad for many reasons. Whenever someone needed something, my family never hesitated to lend a hand and never questioned it. I was mad because the people that always said they were going to be there through thick and thin were never to be found. I woke up June 5, showered, and got ready to go to the hospital. My mom, my sisters, and I sat in the waiting room. We laughed and we cried, until the nurse came out to get my mom prepared for the surgery. The surgery was supposed to last four hours at the most. It lasted about eight because midway through removing her breasts the doctors saw the cancer had spread to her lymph nodes. Finally, my mom was out of surgery, and we were able to see her. Seeing her on the hospital bed was just the beginning of the longest fight we would fight as a family, from my mom losing both her breasts, to having to see her go through so many hard obstacles, to having to prioritize everything.

For the first couple of weeks, my sister and I took turns giving my mom her medication and draining the tubes that were left on her. Family would come over, visit, and bring special food for my mom. It was hard both physically and mentally, but it became more intense when the chemotherapy sessions started. Her hair started falling out, and she became extremely weak. I would cry seeing the change, and my mom would just say, "I'm alive, and everything else is just vanity."

There were times when I wanted to just lay next to my mom, but I couldn't because her immune system was so weak. I just wanted to just be near her, and I couldn't because even a simple cough around her could put her back in the hospital.

The entire journey was like walking into a black tunnel, not knowing when the light was going to shine again. If it wasn't one thing, it was the other, from doctors saying different things to not knowing what would happen next because we had never known anyone who had gone through cancer before. Not only was this experience a physical one, but it was also an emotional and mental one. It was life changing.

I learned to 'Embrace Every Moment,' the good and the bad. I turned everything into a learning experience because deep inside, I believed God puts us through situations for a reason. Two years later, here I am stronger than ever. I'm actually thankful for everything that we went through as a family, helping my mom fight breast cancer. People ask me all the time if I could change one thing what would I change. I always answer that I wouldn't change a thing for the world. I'm completely happy with everything that was thrown my way. I was left with no option other than to embrace every single step of the way.

I learned to never take anything or anyone for granted because you never know what can happen. In a blink of an eye, everything can change. The good moments taught me to enjoy life and to sit back and enjoy the good times and beautiful memories. The bad moments taught me to breathe and to let God handle it all. I had to remember that in order to get to the good, you have to overcome some tough patches in life. It's not always about living in a routine and planning everything out. It's about jumping on a wave and letting the opportunities come. It's about launching on a wave and finding eternity in each moment.

There isn't a day that goes by that I don't tell the people I love that I love them and smile. Embrace Every Moment. You never know how it will turn out in the long run.

About the Author

Karen Ruiz is a small town girl with many hopes and dreams. Her family and friends call her Princess KareBear because of the way she carries herself and the way she loves others. Karen loves to travel and go on adventures. She's all about the memories and the breathtaking views the world has to offer. She is extremely dedicated and never takes no for an answer. She hopes to put her dedication and strong voice to help the youth by becoming a lawyer. She wouldn't be the person she is today if it wasn't for the love and support and prayers from her mother Araceli, father Nahum Ruiz, and her two sisters Daisy and Kelly Ruiz. She lights up any room she walks in with her big smile and laughter.

Bellisima Italia

Elaine M. Tolentino

Travel makes one modest.
You see what a tiny place you occupy in the world."
Gustave Flaubert

When I was in my early twenties, I enjoyed travelling with my friends and family. Whether out of state or overseas, it seemed like no waters were out of reach for our free spirits. One country that I enjoyed visiting was Italy. In September of 2012, my cousin Princess and I embarked on an eight-day Italian adventure, including stops in Rome, Pompeii and Venice. For youngsters like us that enjoy wandering, our motto was "It doesn't have to break the bank." We were on a budget, which made our journey more memorable. We opted for condo-tels instead of franchise hotels for our lodging. We took public transportation instead of booking tours. Most importantly, we strategically scheduled our flights during off-season, which was October.

In a place as momentous as Rome, one does not have to look too far to find amazing art and architecture, especially in places of worship. Luckily, most churches around Rome housed magnificent works of art that one can see free of charge. But, the best thing about traveling is food. Going hungry is one thing no traveler should ever worry about while in Rome. The city is literally flooded with good places to eat. The sidewalk cafes are very popular in Rome.

And when in Rome, you must try an authentic pizza. The best I pizza we had was at Pinsere, located on Termini Street, close to the bus and train stations. You go in and select your pizza from hundreds of toppings. Their combinations were very creative. For example, they offered pumpkin pizza. It was very tasty. It is not like our pan pizza. Their dough is thin and crisp. Pinsere is a small restaurant with standing counters only. The workers were so passionate and had so much energy, which created a very happy and positive atmosphere. It was the best pizza I ever had. The cafes were always populated with happy Italians and a few snooping tourists. It was not out of the ordinary to see Italians.

Outside of eating at the cafe, talking with their friends, and drinking on hot cappuccino, the most important part of our trip, however, was the gelato. We stumbled upon Galateria Della Palma right near the Pantheon and paid about three euro each for two gigantic scoops. There were 150 arrays of flavors to choose from; my favorite was the melon, which tastes exactly like cantaloupe. It's the most amazing gelato I have never tasted and nothing will ever compare again. And, of course, we stopped by the Coliseum, also known as the Flavian Amphitheatre. It was as majestic as I imagined it to be. In the back of my head, I was replaying scenes of the "Gladiator," and jokingly, we were quoting from the movie: "Are you not entertained?" The Coliseum was used for public entertainment, such as gladiator combats and animal matches. I learned from the visit that an earthquake took place in 1349 that collapsed the side of the building. Nonetheless, it was glorious sight!

We also had an opportunity to visit the city of Pompeii by rail. It is around 150 miles south of Rome, an hour and a half bullet train ride. The partially buried Roman town-city of Pompeii is part of a set of five archeological sites in the area. Pompeii was hidden in miles of ash and pumice after the devastating eruption of Mount Vesuvius in 79 A.D. They also made a movie about Pompeii's tragedy. I've traveled and seen plenty of spectacular ruins, but that is one of the finest. The structures, the murals, the paths, the pots, and the bodies- everything is so well preserved. We saw displays of debris with forms of women covering their children- shielding them from the despair that was about to hit them. Also, dogs and other pets were not spared. Even though a lack of maintenance has taken its toll on the place, I still discovered it to be a mesmerizing place to spend the day. One day, I'd love to go back and visit all the buildings again.

The last stop on our itinerary was Venice, a beautiful city located in northeast Italy that is famous for its complex passage system of connected canals. Even though it was pouring cats and dogs when we arrived, the city did not disappoint us. It has been labeled as the most attractive city made by man and one of Europe's most passionate cities. Venice is also famous for its art, design and culture. It was like having a miniature renaissance. The city is still tied to its past. No matter how often one has seen it in photos and films, the real thing is more surreal than one could picture. With canals where streets should be, water shimmers everywhere. The magnificent palaces and churches reflect centuries of history in what was a wealthy trading center. Getting lost in the narrow alleyways is a typical part of exploring Venice. Few places can lay claim to such an impressive natural setting.

Italy's great food, beautiful cities, and extensive history make it an outstanding country to visit. Italy leaves no one underwhelmed, and with so much to do and see, it would take a lifetime to complete. Now that I have a family of my own, I appreciate my excursions more. I am glad that I was able experience Italy before settling down. Travelling brings joy to my life, especially in stressful times. And no matter how uncanny you may think you are, you will find folks on your travels that you just click with. It's a great feeling when you realize that you have so much in common with a person from a distant land! Those amazing travel memories you share will connect you for life.

About the Author

Elaine Tolentino was born and raised in the Philippines and migrated to the United States when she was seventeen. She is the youngest of four siblings. She is a first-time student at College of the Desert, completing an Associate degree in Psychology. She is planning to transfer to a four-year college. She chose psychology as her major because she has a desire to learn more about the human mind and behavior. She hopes to become a clinician someday. She lives in Anza, 56 kilometers Southwest of Palm Desert, CA. She persists to apply the same preciseness to her academic studies as she is with taking care of her family.

Gift of Salvation

for

Non-Believers

"For all have sinned, and come short of the glory of God."
Romans 3:23

This section was written especially for non-believers, those who have not accepted the gift of salvation. The gift of salvation saves souls from eternal damnation and is a free gift offered by God himself. John 3:16-18 says, *"For God so loved the world, that he gave his only begotten Son, that whosoever believeth in him should not perish, but have everlasting life. For God sent not his Son into the world to condemn the world; but that the world through him might be saved. He that believeth on him is not condemned: but he that believeth not is condemned already, because he hath not believed in the name of the only begotten Son of God."* This section of scripture tells us God's purpose for giving His son Jesus to the world. The world was in a bad condition. The world was overwrought with sin; the people were living for fleshly desires rather than for God's desires.

As a result of the world's conditions, God decided that He would offer the perfect sacrifice that would save the world from being a place where people were lost and had no hope. He decided that His own son could stand in proxy for the sin-filled world, taking all sin upon Himself.

So Jesus came, born of a virgin, to save this dying world. He walked on this earth for 33 ½ years, doing the work of His Heavenly Father. At the appointed time, He died by way of crucifixion upon a cross at Calvary, on Golgatha's hill. He shed his blood and died for you and for me. Because His blood was pure, it paid the penalty for all unrighteousness and gave those who believe in Him direct access to His father's throne.

Scripture tells us in Matthew 27:51 that the veil of the temple was ripped in two from top to bottom, at the moment that Jesus' spirit left His body. As a result of the veil's removal, we are no longer required to have a high priest make intercession for us. We, as the children of the Most High God, are able to approach the throne God for ourselves, and Jesus sits on the right hand of the Father making intercession for us.

But what is even more miraculous than God offering His own son as the perfect sacrifice was the fact that when Jesus was placed in grave clothes and placed in a tomb, He only remained there until the third day. God would not have it that His son would remain in the heart of the earth forever. In order for people to believe in the awesome power of God and His dear son Jesus, a miracle had to be performed. So, on the third day, after Jesus died on the cross, He was resurrected, demonstrating the omnipotence of God. This very act was the act that would cause people to believe in a god that reigns supreme and holds the power of the universe in His very hands, a god that could save them from themselves.

Today, if you are an unbeliever, you can change your destiny. You can change where you will spend your eternity. Our Heavenly Father gives us the freedom of choice about how we want to live our life here on earth and how we want to spend eternity. In Deuteronomy 30:19, God boldly declares, *"I call heaven and earth to record this day against you, that I have set before you life and death, blessing and cursing: therefore choose life, that both thou and thy seed may live.*"

So, dear friend what choice will you make today? Will you spend your eternity with the Creator or will you suffer Hell's eternal flames? Again, the choice is yours. Just as the men aboard the ship who were with Jonah became believers, you too can make a choice to accept the only one and true living God as your god.

If after reading the above passages, you have decided that you want to spend your eternity in Heaven with God, the creator, and His son Jesus, and the Holy Spirit, read through what has affectionately come to be known as the Roman's Road. This is the road to salvation. As you read through the scriptures that comprise the Roman's Road, you will also read the explanation for each scripture so you will have clarity about what you are reading and confessing.

The Roman's Road to Salvation

The road to salvation begins with Romans 3:23 which declares, "*For all have sinned, and come short of the glory of God.*" This scripture explains that everyone has come short of God's glory and needs redemption. Then Romans 6:23a states, "*For the wages of sin is death.*" Here, we learn that the consequence of living a life of sin is death. Everyone will experience physical death as a result of the sin committed in the garden of Eden, but those who commit themselves to a life of sin will suffer eternal damnation in the lake of fire (Rev. 19).

Continue with the rest of verse 6:23 that says, "*but the gift of God is eternal life through Jesus Christ our Lord.*" There is an alternative to suffering eternal damnation. We can accept the gift of salvation by accepting Jesus as our personal lord and savior. Then, Romans 5:8 says, "*But God commendeth his love toward us, in that, while we were yet sinners, Christ died for us.*" We are able to receive the gift of salvation because Christ came to earth and shed His blood for us on the cross.

Continue to Romans 10: 9-10 which says, *"That if thou shalt confess with thy mouth the Lord Jesus, and shalt believe in thine heart that God hath raised him from the dead, thou shalt be saved. For with the heart man believeth unto righteousness; and with the mouth confession is made unto salvation."* If we confess with our mouths that Jesus is the son of God, that he came and died for our sins, and that God raised Him from the dead, we will receive salvation.

Finish with Romans 10:13, which states, *"For whosoever shall call upon the name of the Lord shall be saved."* Call upon the name of God by saying these words, **"Lord Jesus, come into my heart and save me Lord. I believe that you are the Son of God who came and died on the cross for my sins. I believe that you rose from the grave. I also believe that you now sit in heaven on the right side of the Father, making intersession for me. I accept you as my Lord and my Savior."**

Now that you have confessed with your mouth that Jesus is the son of God and that He died for our sins and rose from the grave, **YOU ARE NOW SAVED!!!!** You will spend your eternity in heaven.

The next step is very important- you must find a bible-based church that teaches the word of God and confesses the Lord Jesus Christ to be the son of God. Don't delay. Do this immediately. Do not leave yourself open to the enemy. Get connected with the saints of the Most High God and keep yourself covered with the unspotted blood of the lamb.

Here is my prayer for you.

Father God,

I thank you for the opportunity to minister your word to the unsaved, the unchurched, and the uncommitted. Father God, I pray now for the souls who have just received the gift of salvation. Lord Father, they have opened their hearts to you, and I know that you have received them into your kingdom and written their names in the Book of Life. Father God, I pray that you will touch their lives and show yourself mightily before them. Let their eyes be opened by the scales falling off, allowing them to see clearly.

Father God, I even pray for the backslider, those who have turned away from you after receiving the gift of salvation. You said in your word that you desire that none would perish. So Lord, I send your word to them right now praying that they would confess the iniquity in their heart, repent, and turn from their evil ways, so that they may receive a life of abundance. You said in your word in Matthew Chapter 14, that every knee shall bow before you and every tongue will confess that Jesus is Lord.

Father God, I pray now that we all come under subjection to your word and that we will humbly submit our lives to you. I ask all these things in the name of my Lord and Savior Jesus Christ. Amen, Amen, Amen!!!!

I will continue to pray for your success in your walk with God. Remember, this spiritual walk that you are about to embark on will not be an easy walk, but remember, the race is not given to the swift but to those who endure to the end.

Be blessed with heaven's best. I love you!

About the Editor

Dr. Cassundra White-Elliott resides in California with her family, where as an English/Education professor she works for various community colleges and universities.

When writing, she writes with the direction of the Holy Spirit, in an effort to share with God's people all that He has for them.

In addition to teaching and writing, Dr. White-Elliott also serves as an evangelistic teacher. She is also the founder of International Women's Commission, a ministry that serves the needs of the entire person, by attending to healing the mind, body, soul, and spirit.

Dr. White-Elliott holds a Ph.D. in Education, a Master's in English Composition, and a Bachelor's in Education.

Dr. White-Elliott is also the founder of CLF Publishing, LLC. For your publishing needs, go online to www.clfpublishing.org.

A Mother's Heart

Edited by: **Dr. Cassundra White-Elliott**

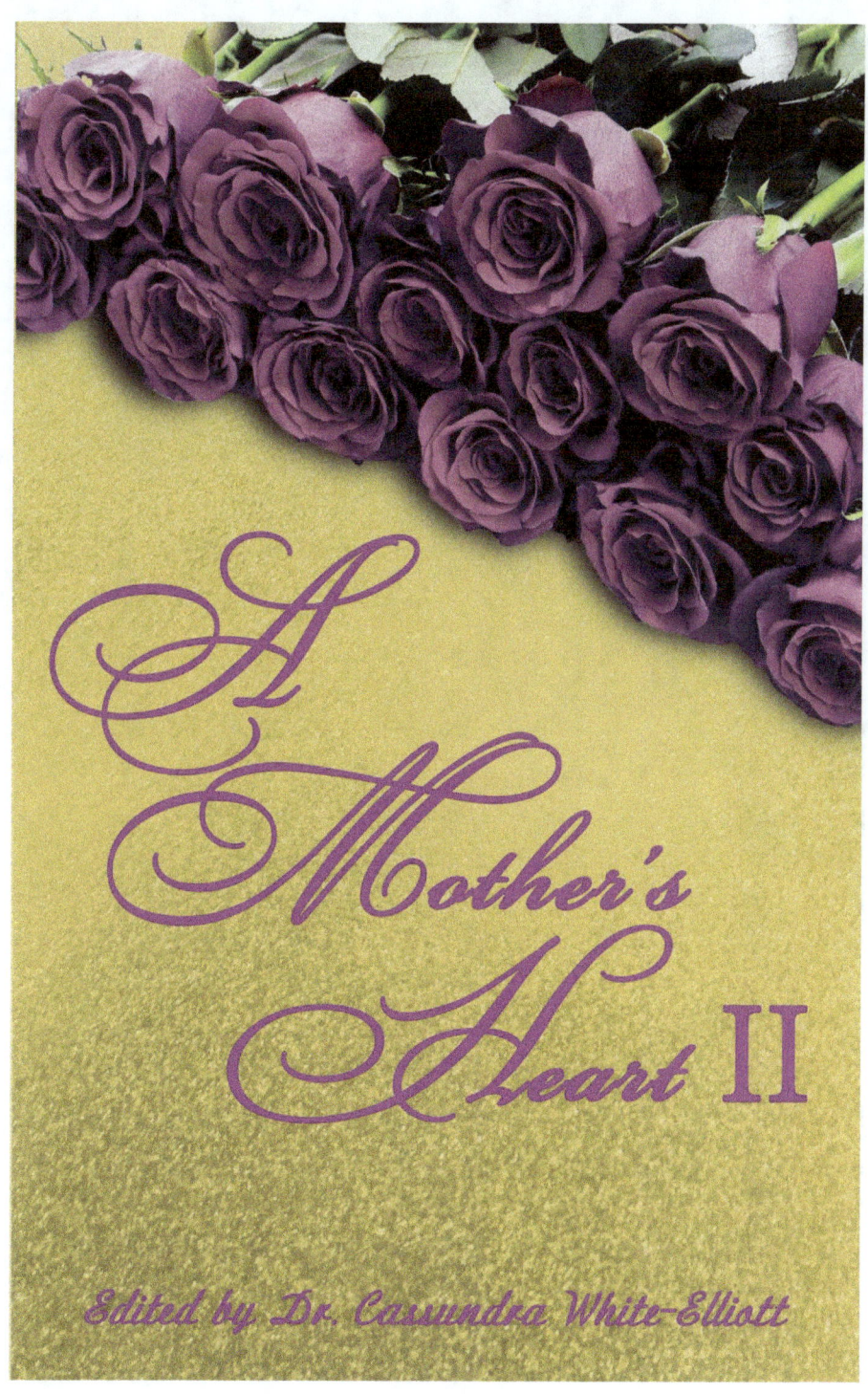

A Mother's Heart II

Edited by Dr. Cassundra White-Elliott

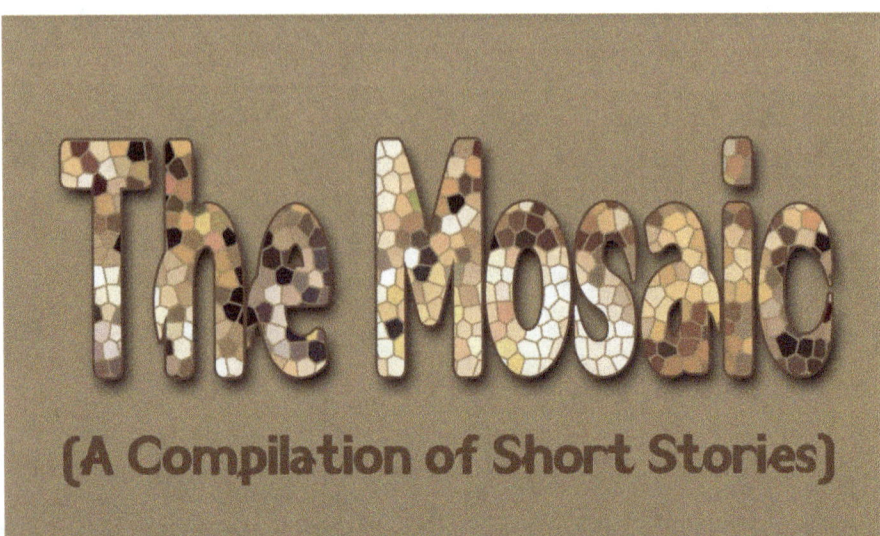

The Mosaic

(A Compilation of Short Stories)

Edited by *Dr. C. White-Elliott*

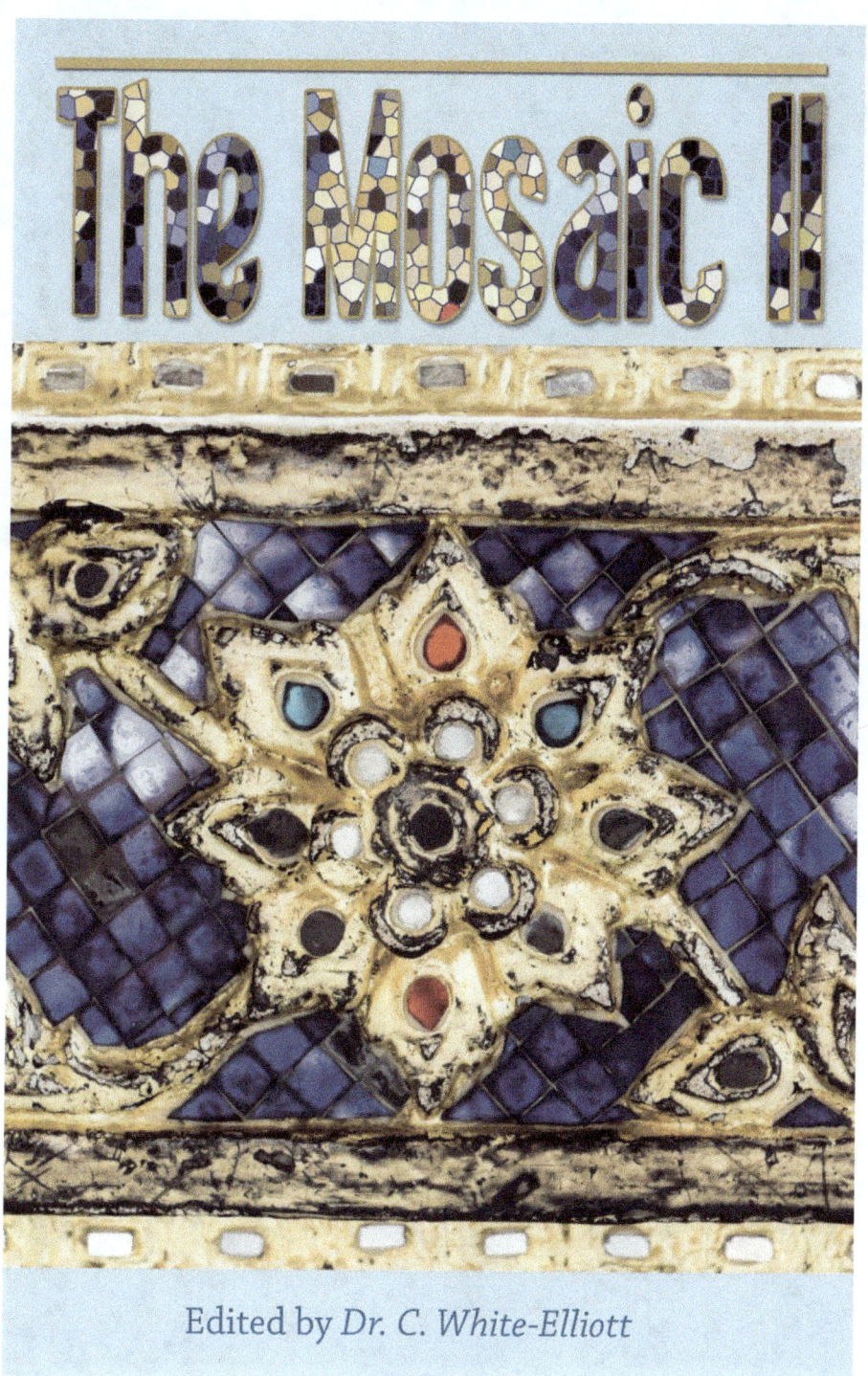

The Mosaic II

Edited by *Dr. C. White-Elliott*

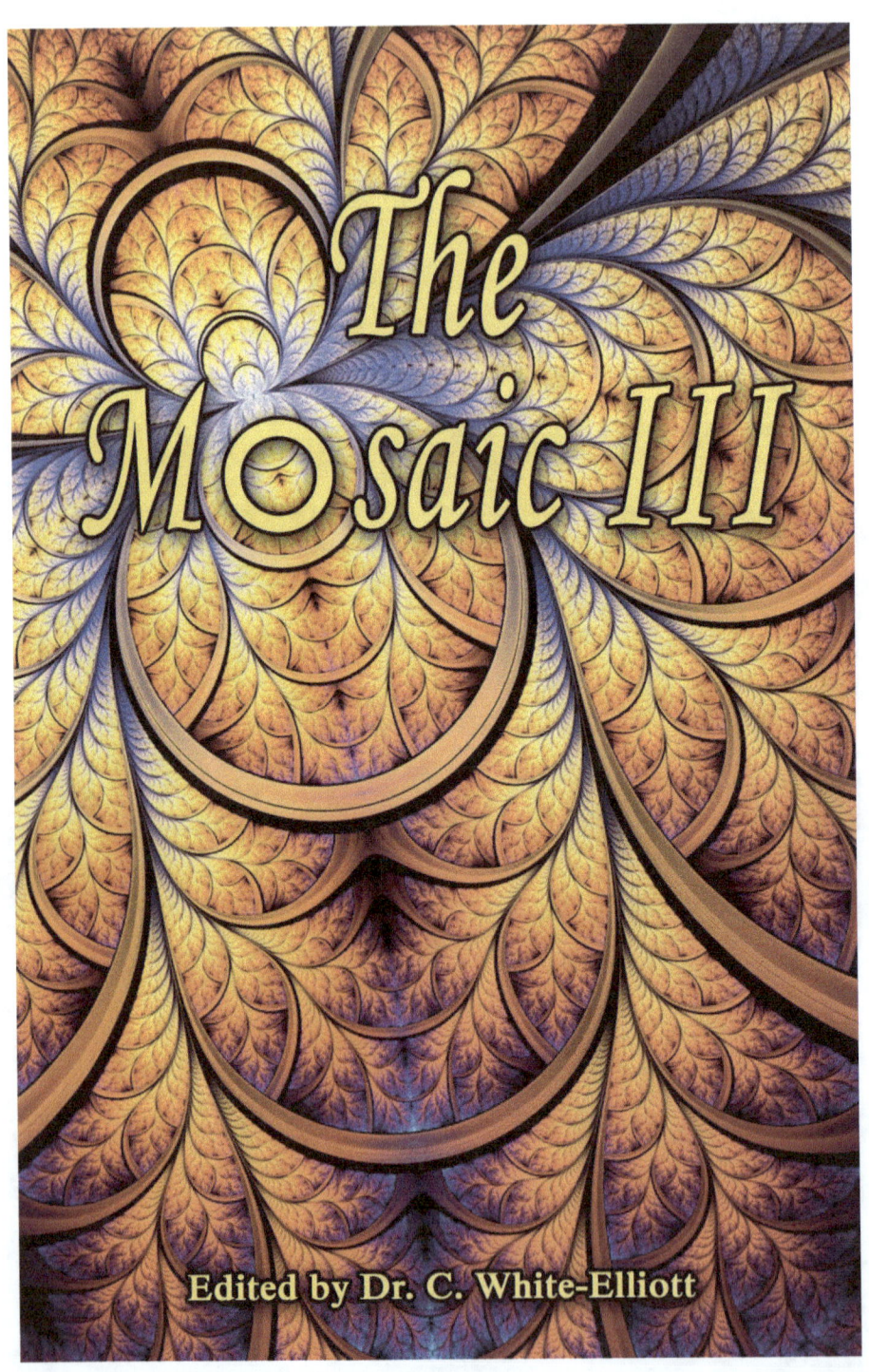

The Mosaic III

Edited by Dr. C. White-Elliott

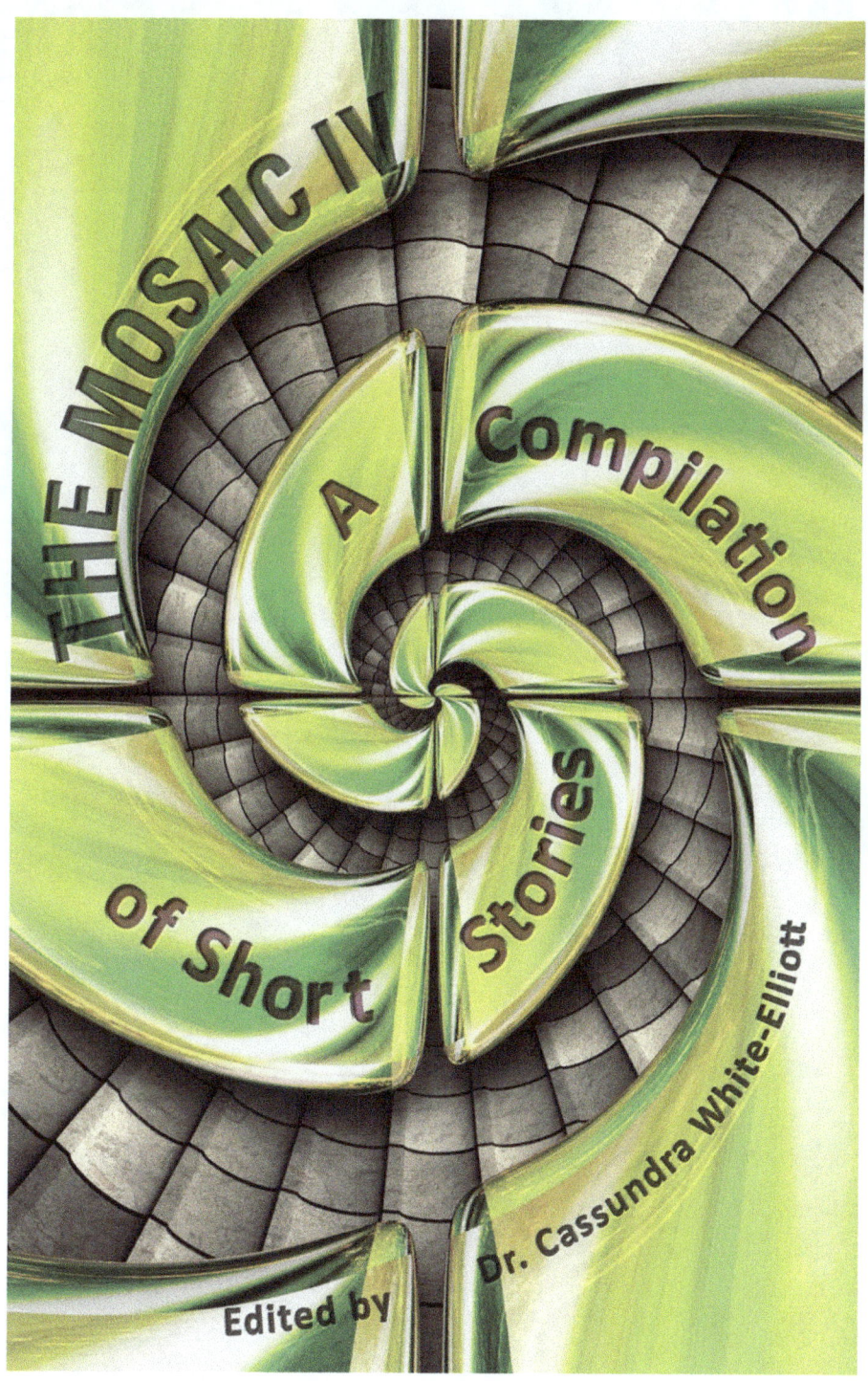

THE MOSAIC IV

A Compilation of Short Stories

Edited by Dr. Cassundra White-Elliott

www.ingramcontent.com/pod-product-compliance
Lightning Source LLC
Chambersburg PA
CBHW051835020726
47502CB00005B/1800

* 9 7 8 1 9 4 5 1 0 2 1 7 2 *